SAVED BY HIM

NEW PLEASURES BOOK 3

M. S. PARKER

BELMONTE PUBLISHING, LLC

READING ORDER

Thank you so much for reading Saved by Him, the final book in the New Pleasures series. If you'd like to read the complete series, I recommend reading them in this order:

ONE

"I TOLD YOU WHAT I WANT, BUT IT DOESN'T CHANGE THAT
you're hurt."

"It's too bad. Because that means I'll have to lay down on
that nice comfy bed and make myself feel better."

Pain. Darkness. Fear.

Every pull of his mouth went straight to my clit, and I
writhed under the heavy weight of his body. Skin and muscle,
friction and pressure. So, so, so good.

Metal and copper. Dirt and mildew. A faint medicinal
taste under all of it.

"J, J," I whimpered. "I need more. Harder, please. More."

"I've got you." His lips brushed across mine. "I've got you,
Rona, and I'm not going to lose you again."

Lost. Lost. Drifting in darkness. Surrounded by darkness.
Cold. Cold.

His hips jerked upward, driving into me with the exact
right amount of force to push me toward climax.

Head throbbing. Muscles aching. None of it with pleasant associations.

Being blindfolded required trust, handing over control, and that was what he was offering me. His trust, his control. The blindfold in his hands.

Thick darkness. Suffocating. Each gasp of air was work.

He stretched out beneath me, all tanned skin and rippling muscles. I could spend hours tracing every dip and plane with my tongue. Maybe later I would, but right now, I needed him inside me again.

My mouth was dry, my tongue swollen. The nasty taste made me want to spit, but I didn't have any saliva in my mouth.

He groaned as I lowered myself onto his thick shaft, his hands flexing on my hips.

"I want to see you," he said as I dropped down until he was completely sheathed inside me. "Gorgeous tits and those china-blue eyes. Please, Rona, let me see you."

My temples throbbed in time with my heartbeat, and as muddled as I was, I could tell it was sluggish. This wasn't a hangover.

I rocked back and forth, letting my body adjust. My hands went to my breasts, fingers teasing my nipples until they were hard little points. I tugged on them, the jolt of pain making me moan.

Pain in my wrists. My ankles. A different pain in my head. Something beyond the thick, stuffy feeling.

He surged upward, keeping on the blindfold even as his arms went around my waist. He pulled me tight against his chest, the hair there chafing my nipples in a way that made me want to squirm. But I couldn't. His embrace was unbreakable.

I tried to move, but I couldn't. My limbs were weighed down. Heavy. Restricted. But I didn't feel safe, not like I did when he had me underneath him, his body essentially pinning me in place.

I whimpered as he bit the side of my neck. I'd never known that there was a part of pain that could be pleasurable, not until Jalen Larsen came into my life. His blunt nails scratched across my back, not doing any damage, but sending little pricks of near-pain running across my nerves.

The fog was starting to lift from my mind, giving way to a clarity that I suddenly didn't want. It was better to stay with Jalen in my mind. When I knew what was happening, I couldn't unknow it. The knowledge would always be there, and whatever it was, I didn't want it.

"I love you," he whispered against my lips. *"You're my home, Rona. The only woman I want, the only one I'll ever want. Nothing can change that. Not even–"*

The baby.

Shit.

Jalen's supposed-to-be-ex-wife, Elise Marx, was pregnant. And Jalen was the father. So she said.

I didn't want to be one of those women who automatically took her man's side. The sort who assumed women were lying or that if a man was cheating, it was the other woman's fault. Not that what happened between Jalen and Elise had been cheating. It happened before Jalen and I even met. And what was happening between Jalen and me wasn't cheating either. He wasn't the one dragging his feet in the divorce.

All of this came rushing into my mind in one nearly overwhelming flood, making my head spin. I didn't try to stop it though. As much as I wanted to go back to that dream world where Jalen and I were making love, I knew this was more important because this was real. The first part of my half-dream had been based on reality. After sex, Jalen told me that he wanted me to blindfold him, a display of trust that had made my heart race. We hadn't done it, though, because it was at that moment that Elise had come barging into the house with her news.

I'd left, I remembered suddenly.

Jalen had demanded a paternity test, saying that he didn't believe the child was his, a statement that had reminded me of my father's accusations of infidelity against my mother. I'd gotten my head on straight about that though. Jalen had caught Elise literally in the act of having sex with another man. His doubts regarding who she'd been sleeping with were completely founded.

But I'd still left. Why? I hadn't been angry at Jalen, and my feelings about Elise were…multi-layered. I'd been invited into the house, asked to stay. Elise hadn't. Even though Jalen had clearly wanted to talk through this with her, he hadn't asked me to leave. I'd done it on my own.

Another memory clicked into place.

I'd wanted to give them time and space to work out all the ways their lives were about to change. And I wanted some space of my own. I hadn't broken up with Jalen, but I had told him that I needed time to figure out how he would fit into my life differently now that he had a baby on the way.

Cold. Damn cold. Not surprising considering it was the beginning of December in Colorado. Snow in the mountains could come year-round. With Christmas on the way, I was surprised I hadn't been snowed in yet.

I was cold because I'd been walking. I called for a car, but

I hadn't wanted to stay at the house with Elise and Jalen while I waited.

There'd been a car, I remembered. No, not a car, a van. A dark van.

Someone had gotten out of it.

I gagged, the memory of a damp cloth, the same sickly-sweet smell that was now coating my tongue. Shit. Chloroform. The name didn't matter though. What mattered was that my brain had finally caught up to my surroundings.

I'd been kidnapped.

Someone had literally knocked me out and taken me somewhere against my will.

Saying it a different way didn't make it any less surreal. What the fuck?!

I let myself have a few seconds to panic, and then I forced myself to focus. I hadn't gotten through hell with my father only to die here, alone, tied up in the dark. I'd lived through nearly being eviscerated. I would live through this.

With that thought in mind, I took inventory.

My head hurt, but it didn't feel like I was bleeding from anywhere. I didn't remember hitting my head. That was good. It meant I didn't need to worry about a concussion or anything like that. My headache was just the after-effect of the chloroform. Unless whoever had taken me had dropped me on the floor, and I'd hit my head then.

I opened my eyes, but it didn't make a difference. I really hoped it was because wherever I'd been stashed was dark and not because I was blind. My eyes didn't hurt, but if I'd gotten hit hard enough... no, I refused to consider that. It was just dark in here.

That was fact number one. Fact number two was that my

hands and feet were tied. Based on the lack of give and how sticky it felt, I was going with duct tape. I knew how to get out of it. I'd been one of the best in my class when it came to escaping various kinds of restraints. I needed to evaluate my situation more before I decided whether it would be advantageous to have my hands free or not.

I'd probably have only one shot at escaping, and I didn't want to ruin it because I got impatient.

I wasn't gagged, which meant I was most likely stashed somewhere isolated or soundproofed, maybe both. If they were worried I could attract attention, they would've gagged me even while I was out. Which meant screaming wouldn't do any good, even if it might've made me feel better.

I cleared my throat, then coughed. The sound didn't echo, but it wasn't flat either. My gut told me that I was in a room, but not a huge one. No windows. I put my hand on the ground and felt something smooth, cold. Probably tile or concrete. Same with the walls. It reinforced my thought that I was in a basement.

Wonderful.

TWO

I WOULD'VE THOUGHT THAT THE WORST PART OF BEING tied up in a pitch-black room was not being able to move, but that wasn't it. At least not yet. When I needed to pee, I was sure I'd change my mind, but for right now, the fact that I couldn't tell how much time had passed was driving me crazy.

I'd left Jalen's place sometime in the late afternoon, early evening. I had no idea how long I'd been unconscious, and because there were no windows, I couldn't tell what time of day it was. Was it still Thursday or was it Friday already?

It couldn't be any later than Friday because I hadn't wet myself, though the pressure in my lower belly indicated that might not be the case soon. I was hungry and thirsty, but I could ignore my stomach for a while. Dehydration would kill me before hunger.

Kill me.

Fuck.

I could die here.

No. I shook my head. No, I wouldn't die here. Not like this. Not when I had...

A half sob caught in my throat as Jalen's face flashed through my mind. Rich brown hair, brilliant turquoise eyes, the sort of face that could only be described as ruggedly handsome. Six-four, with broad shoulders and muscles that weren't just for show.

After everything Jalen and I had been through, it couldn't end like this. We'd just said, "I love you" and, sure, this thing with Elise was going to make things tense, but I wanted us to get through it. I wanted us to work through everything, to build a relationship.

Everything I hadn't thought I'd want, a life that I'd never pictured myself having, I saw it all now. I saw it with Jalen. A life. A family.

But only if I got out of here.

I had to be smart though.

More time passed, but it could have been minutes or hours. I shifted myself around until I was sitting. At some point, I figured out how to tug down my pants and relieved myself in a corner. Not the high point of my day, but considering the rest of my situation, it wasn't the lowest either.

That's what I had to prepare myself for. The lowest. The worst. The things that, as a former student of the FBI, I knew could be coming. It all depended on who had me and why.

If they were looking for a ransom, they probably wouldn't hurt me, especially if it was Jalen they were going to try to ransom me to. Except I doubted that was the case since not many people knew the two of us were together.

Which meant it might be a random kidnapping. That wouldn't be good. Adult women weren't generally kidnapped by grieving mothers to replace a child. I'd done enough psychological work to know that a quick death would probably be the best outcome I could hope for.

But there was one other possibility.

My father.

Any time in the last few years, I wouldn't have been thinking about him at all, but ever since the second trial, he hadn't been ignoring me like before. In fact, he'd been trying to talk to me. I'd kept getting collect calls from him, or at least I had before he'd escaped.

Had my father arranged this? Was this his way of trying to control me from where ever he'd escaped to?

The sad thing was, that possibility might be the best shot I'd have at making it out of here alive and unscathed. My father would want to take care of things himself. He wouldn't want anyone else to kill me. Since he was most likely hiding somewhere closer to Indiana, that would be a problem. Which meant now that they had me, they had to figure out what to do with me while they waited. That meant I had time.

Suddenly, a burst of light from the other side of the room blinded me. I cursed, holding up my hands in front of my face while blinking until my eyes adjusted. I heard a click, and an overhead light came on. It was a single, dingy bulb, but offered enough light for me to finally see my surroundings... and wish that I hadn't.

Cinderblock walls covered with peeling gray paint. A concrete floor, smooth but not finished. A cinderblock ceiling with the lone bulb that looked ready to blow.

This wasn't a normal basement. Normal basements had wooden or tiled ceilings. Unless we were in a warehouse or something similar, a basement like this had to be purposefully made, and I could only think of one reason why someone would do that.

To hold someone like me.

I resisted the urge to check closer, to look for signs that other women had been held here. It wasn't hard to do, really, since a large, muscular man was now standing directly in front of me, a glower on his square-jawed face. Buzz-cut brown hair and ice-cold eyes all gave me the impression of one of those Soviet villains from eighties' movies. Like the big guy in *Rocky*.

This was bad. Really bad.

I'd assumed that my father would've hired some scrawny, wiry ex-con who needed chloroform to take me down. This guy was big enough that, no matter how tough I knew I could be, he could've taken me down without drugs. It would've been messy, dangerous, and time-consuming, though, because I sure as hell wouldn't have gone quietly.

"What's up?" I grinned up at him, not bothering to hide the anger I felt. Instead of playing the helpless, weak woman, I was going for disarming with bluntness. I'd never been any good at pretending to be a damsel in distress, anyway. I wasn't even going to try.

His eyes slid away from me for a moment, and then he sneered.

Shame flooded me as I realized he knew I'd had to urinate in my little cell. I hadn't done anything wrong, or anything that I'd really had any control over, but I was still ashamed. I pushed the embarrassment down, knowing that my cheeks were still burning. I squared my shoulders and lifted my chin.

"When you gotta go." I shrugged. "Maybe you should've given me a bucket."

His hand flashed out, the back of it cracking against my cheek and jaw in an explosion of pain. My head snapped to the side, and I hissed out a breath of air. Fortunately, it was far from the most painful thing I'd ever experienced, and it took only seconds for my thoughts to gather again.

"How is my father planning on getting here?" I gently touched the back of my hand to my cheek. "I know he'll want to take care of me himself."

The man's expression didn't change as he reached down and grabbed the front of my shirt. He yanked me upright and slammed me against the wall. It didn't feel great, but I wasn't going to let it show. In fact, I couldn't resist taunting him a bit.

"How's it feel to have an old man yanking your leash like some—"

All the air rushed out of me as he buried his fist in my stomach. I curled forward, coughing and retching as I tried to stay on my feet. I hadn't expected a punch to the stomach. A backhand to the face, sure, but I figured that was to let me know it was a good idea to do as I was told.

"You are a problem."

His English was impeccable. That combined with the military haircut and the way he carried himself made me suspect U.S. military, but probably first generation from an immigrant family. My gut – aching as it was – still said something Soviet. Not that it mattered right now.

"I know." I sounded a bit breathless, but not too bad. "My dad thought I was such a problem that he tried to kill me. It didn't take."

The man frowned, his forehead creasing. "Why do you keep talking about your father? I have no interest in your family. Not yet, anyway. If you continue to be problematic for my employers, they may wish to meet your father."

Shit.

Not random. Not ransom. Not my father.

What the fuck was going on then?

I didn't let my confusion show on my face, forcing my tone to stay light. "That might be difficult for them since he's on the run now."

Not a flicker. Either he'd already known about my father, or he simply didn't care. Most likely the latter.

The man grabbed my hair and yanked my head back, giving me no choice but to look up at him. "I won't mark your face again."

I didn't have to wonder what he meant by that because his fist collided with my ribcage even as the last word came out. I gasped, choked, but I couldn't catch my breath because his hand was around my throat now, squeezing. I pushed against his chest with my bound hands, but there was no strength in me. Black spots danced in my vision, and my knees gave out, but I didn't fall.

He was silent as he hit me again, but I couldn't hear the impact over the blood rushing in my ears. He must have been counting, or he knew how long he could choke and beat me until it was too much, because he suddenly stopped.

I dropped to the floor, but I barely felt my knees hit. I was sure it hurt, but everything else hurt too much for me to really notice. I supposed I'd see the bruises... if I survived this first. And judging by the way I was feeling at this moment, *not* surviving could be a viable option.

Except he wasn't trying to kill me. He could have, I knew that. Even with as much pain and oxygen deprivation that my brain was trying to handle, I knew that things could have been much worse.

They could still get worse.

I had to get through the pain, figure out where I was, and how I could get out.

"Serge."

A scrawny guy burst into the room and didn't even look twice at me. He muttered something in another language, and the big guy – Serge, I supposed – snapped something back in that same language. Judging by the way the little guy scurried away, Serge was the top dog. Here, anyway. He'd mentioned bosses.

I sucked in another burning breath. Bosses. Who the *hell* in my circle of people would have *bosses* that would want me beaten up?

Serge leaned over me, and a part of me wanted to kick him, hurt him the way he'd hurt me, but I knew that if I did, I'd get another beating. That one might knock me out, and if I was unconscious, I couldn't keep working on the problem of my escape.

"If you are not a problem, we will not need to have this discussion again." He straightened and put his hands in his pockets. "Someone will bring you food once you are well enough to eat."

The fact that he knew that I wouldn't be able to keep anything down until the pain dissipated told me that I wasn't the first person he'd beaten like this.

The question I wasn't sure I wanted answered was, how many of those people had died here?

THREE

He left the light on, and while I wanted to think that he was being kind, I doubted it. Serge didn't strike me as the sort of person who did things out of the kindness of his heart. He'd done it for some reason. Maybe to show that if I was agreeable, things wouldn't be so bad.

As if anything that happened in this room wouldn't be bad.

I still didn't have windows, but I felt like I could better judge the passage of time this way. While I didn't know what day it was, or even what time of day, I was confident that only a few hours had passed before the door opened again.

Then again, that could've had less to do with light and more to do with the fact that the pain in my torso had lessened but not completely faded. It wasn't Serge this time, but I didn't lower my guard as the scrawny guy from before brought a paper cup and plate over to me. Just because someone wasn't big didn't mean they couldn't be vicious.

My father was proof of that.

The guy set the food and drink down in front of me, removed the tape from my wrists and rattled something off in what sounded like Russian but wasn't quite Russian. Croatian maybe. Or Romanian. One of those countries that had been part of the Soviet Union before it dissolved. I did know some Russian. I wouldn't have needed it as much as an FBI agent as I would have if I'd been trying to make it into the CIA, but I'd studied it along with Spanish, French, and Korean. Spanish was the only one I'd really been any good at, but I knew enough Russian to know that it wasn't what this guy was speaking.

"Thank you." I shifted around, not bothering to hide my winces of pain as I moved. If I let this guy think I was weaker than I was, I might be able to use it in the future, either to catch him off-guard or to play him and Serge off each other.

For the first time in a while, I wished I'd made it further at Quantico.

"Welcome." The word was heavily accented, but now I knew that he understood at least some English, probably more than he let on.

Filing that away under possibly useful information, I turned my attention to the food in front of me. Despite how much I was hurting, my stomach growled. I forced myself to take a small sip of water first and was pleasantly surprised to find it cool and clean. The food was a simple peanut butter and jelly sandwich and an apple, but the fruit wasn't rotten, and the bread wasn't moldy. I hoped that meant they cared whether I got sick. I took my time eating, in part to keep myself from throwing up if my body decided it didn't want to accept food just yet, but it was more about having something to do.

After I finished, I leaned back against the wall and wrapped my arms around my knees, holding them close enough to let me rest my head. The light was still on, and I found myself able to relax. Well, as much as anyone could relax in this sort of situation. I let my mind wander rather than forcing it to start looking for ways out. The food had given me some energy, but I needed some non-chemical-induced rest. I doubted I'd be able to sleep, but if I could rest for a couple hours, I'd be thinking a lot more clearly.

Forcing my mind away from my current circumstances, of course, meant that my thoughts went to Jalen. I hated how we left things, and I hoped that he didn't think I was ignoring him because of Elise. Then again, maybe that was better. If he knew I'd been taken, he'd be out of his mind trying to find me and feeling helpless when he couldn't. I hoped that if he did know I was gone, he'd go to Clay, or at least to Jenna, who'd bring Clay in on things. It wasn't that I trusted Clay more, but he'd been trained in this sort of thing, and he had resources that Jalen didn't. If Jalen had been able to find a missing person, we never would have met...

I'd been hoping for a white Christmas, I thought as I stood in front of the window and watched the snow fall in thick, wet flakes that promised even more accumulation. Now I was thinking that I might've been hoping too hard. It was a snow emergency. Non-essential businesses were closed, and the schools would have been too if they hadn't already been on break for the holidays. People were being told to stay off the roads unless absolutely necessary, and snowplows could barely keep up around the hospitals and emergency services.

Muscled arms slid around my waist and pulled me back

against a broad chest. I rested my head on Jalen's shoulder with a sigh.

"Do you think Santa's going to be able to make it through all this snow?" Jalen's breath was hot against my skin, and I shivered. He tightened his embrace. "If he does, are you expecting something special in your stocking this year?"

My mind immediately flashed back to the previous year when Jalen had dressed up like Santa and crawled into bed late Christmas Eve, a ring box in hand. I didn't think Jalen could top that, but I was pretty sure I could.

Before I could spoil the surprise, I turned around and coiled my arms around his neck, pushing up on my toes to brush my mouth across his. "That depends," I said. "Is Santa going to give me what I asked for?"

"And what was that?" Jalen's lips curved into a sensual smile.

"A handsome man, all trussed up and blindfolded, wearing only a bow."

"I think that can be arranged even if Old Saint Nick can't make it here." Jalen's hands slid down from the small of my back to my ass, each one cupping a cheek for a moment before he gave me two quick smacks.

I made a pleased sound and ground my hips against his, smiling as I felt his erection pushing at my stomach.

"Are you sure you've been a good girl this year?" The wicked grin he gave me said he'd already decided which list I'd made.

I shook my head. "Not at all. But I don't want coal in my stocking."

"Do you think I can come up with a better punishment

than that?" His grip on my ass loosened, and a moment later, his hand moved underneath my silky pajama shorts.

"Yes, please," I breathed, my eyes closing. In the time we'd been together, he'd introduced me to all sorts of delightful punishments.

Spankings, of course, sometimes with his hand, sometimes with a belt or flogger. Orgasm denial. He'd once kept me on the edge for two exquisite hours, begging and sobbing for him to let me tip over the edge. On the opposite end, last year, he'd given me a pair of panties that had a vibrator that fit right against my clit, then had me wear them to a party Jenna and Rylan had thrown. He'd practically had to carry me out by the end of the night. Then there was...

I gasped as he pushed a finger into my ass. Yeah, there was that too. Anal wasn't always a punishment, but he could make it be one. I grabbed the front of his shirt and buried my face against his chest as he worked his finger in and out, the dry friction burning even more than usual.

"How do you want it?" he asked, teeth scraping the top of my ear. "Up against the window? Bent over the chair? In the playroom, on your back, legs in the air?"

All of them sounded wonderful, but at that moment, one choice stood out. "I want to watch the snow."

He nodded. Without missing a stroke, he backed us up until I could feel the chill from the glass. He claimed my mouth with a harsh, bruising kiss, his tongue plundering my mouth, exploring every inch of it. I was breathless by the time it broke, barely noticing as he spun me around and pressed me against the glass. My silk shirt did little to protect my skin from the cold, my nipples immediately pebbling. He tugged *down my shorts until they dropped the rest of the way on their own, then he kicked my legs apart.*

"I hope you're ready, because this is going to hurt."

The voice registered a second after the words, and I screamed. That wasn't Jalen behind me. Not his hands on my hips. Not him pushing his way inside me. I didn't know who it was, but it wasn't Jalen.

I screamed again, but I couldn't hear myself. All I could hear was laughter and the loud grunts of the man forcing himself into my body.

This wasn't real. It couldn't be real. It was a nightmare. It had to be.

I needed to wake up.

I knew the world I was waking up to was bad, but this was worse. There, the bad was limited to reality. Here, my imagination had no limits.

And I didn't know if I could survive them.

FOUR

I WAS SCREAMING WHEN I JERKED OUT OF MY nightmare, my throat straining, burning. My lungs were on fire, screaming for oxygen, but my ribs protested every movement, racking my entire body with pain. Choking, gasping, I tasted blood in the back of my throat, and I remembered the last time I'd felt like this, unable to breathe, my mouth filled with my own blood.

"Shut up!"

I sucked in another breath and gagged, coughed. I wasn't yelling anymore, but I wasn't exactly quiet either. It was hard to be quiet when I felt like I was coughing up a lung.

"Shut up!"

Suddenly, I was off the floor and being slammed into the wall. The little bit of air I'd managed to get rushed out, leaving me gaping like a fish and wondering if I was going to pass out. Serge put his face right in front of mine, his eyes icy.

"I told you that if you behaved, we would not need to talk

again." His voice had dropped from shouting to something flat and much, much scarier.

He was going to hurt me again, and this time, it wouldn't end with me in pain, but I'd be broken. Probably dead. I didn't want to be dead. I needed to convince him that I would be quiet.

But I didn't *want* to be quiet. If he was going to kill me, then I sure as hell would go down fighting. I hit out with my bound hands, catching him on the chin. His head snapped back, then slowly came down, his expression stony.

"Let me go!" I twisted, trying to get free, trying to kick him. All reason had fled. I wasn't thinking like an FBI trainee, methodically trying to break free. I was scrambling, desperate.

I didn't want to die. Not now. Not like this.

I hadn't survived my father to die like this.

"Stop."

He shook me, and my head bounced off the wall. Pain shot through my skull and sent stars flashing in front of my eyes.

Serge shouted something over his shoulder, seeming oblivious to my feet bouncing off his massive thighs. I wondered if he felt anything at all. Pain. Excitement. My nightmare came back, and I knew I'd prefer violence to excitement.

"The first time was a lesson," Serge said. "But my employers will be upset if you are marked up."

Oh shit.

That didn't sound good.

Shit. *Shit.*

"Why not?" I asked. "Why will they be upset?"

I was still trying to squirm, but I was rapidly losing strength. A sandwich and a couple hours of sleep were no match for what I'd been through. I'd thought I could handle it because I'd spent nearly three months at Quantico. What a joke.

I was a joke, thinking I could do something.

The scrawny guy came running in, carrying something in his hand. I couldn't see what it was, but I had a feeling I wasn't going to like it.

Serge dropped me to the floor, then crouched down next to me. "I had hoped you would be a smart one, learn from your introduction that it would be better to let things happen." He shook his head and held out his hand to the other guy. "But since you decided to be problematic, I must now do something I don't want to do."

My eyes widened. He'd had no problem beating me. How bad did it have to be if he didn't want to do it?

I cursed as something sharp pierced my arm. I looked down even though I knew what I'd see. A syringe sticking out of my arm.

"What the fuck?!" I tried to jerk my arm away, but I knew it was too late. Whatever had been in the syringe was now in my bloodstream.

Wonderful.

***

THE CEILING WAS SWIRLING.

Round and round and round. Bright colors. Shiny colors.

I liked the colors. The room was better with the colors. Instead of gray, they were red and green and blue and silver and orange. Swirling like circles and triangles.

I shifted on the floor, and the swirls went with me. That was new too. I liked it. Before, when it had been dark, I'd been bored. It wasn't dark now, and I wasn't bored. I was playing tick-tack-toe with the swirls.

Green won first and got cocky. Red didn't like that and got distracted. I beat red and then played yellow. Yellow cheated by putting a unicorn in the center, and that was when things got crazy. The colors took sides and then everything else started fighting too.

The triangles on my wrists hurt so I rubbed them together until the triangles turned into rectangles, and I threw them away. I pumped my fists in the air and cheered on the buffalos until I fell asleep.

Running. Running. It was dark, and the trees were scary, but they weren't chasing me. They cheered, yelling bad words and things in other languages that I couldn't understand. I wanted to tell them to talk to me or stop yelling, but I was having a hard time breathing. My sides hurt. I was out of shape. But I shouldn't be out of shape. I ran all the time. Lifted weights. Boxed.

But it hurt to breathe. Ribs and stomach hurt too. Why?

It was hard to run, not just to breathe. My feet felt funny. Tingly numb, like I'd sat on them.

Whoever was chasing me needed to stop because I couldn't run anymore.

I was too tired.

I turned...and screamed...

My eyes popped open, and I stared around the room. The colors were gone, but *he* was still there.

Standing against the wall. Those dark eyes boring into me. Watching me. Daring me.

"Get away from me!"

I held out my hands, pointed at him.

"He shouldn't be here. He shouldn't be here. He's not here. No. Not here. Can't be here."

He took a step forward, and I scrambled backward, my head thumping against the wall. It hurt, but I didn't care because he couldn't be here.

"No. No. No. You're not here. You're not here."

I shook my head, then dug my hands into my hair. I closed my eyes, pulled my hair. He had to go away. He wasn't here. Not here. I never had to see him again. Never again.

"Look at me, Rona." His familiar voice cracked and warbled. "Look at your father. Don't be a bad girl. Look at me."

"No, no. I'm not hearing you. You're not here. Go away."

"I'm here, and I'm going to finish what I started."

"No!" The word ripped out of me, and I screamed it again and again until the colors came and wrapped me up.

They were soft and nice. They invited me to play again. Hangman this time. I said yes. I was always good at hangman. I liked words. I always thought of great words that no one ever guessed.

Quixotic.

Lackadaisical.

Ambiance.

Chivalrous.

People were always surprised at that last one, like no one ever thought about chivalry anymore. I supposed it was as dead as everyone said. Dead as I wished *he* was.

But he wasn't dead.

Green nudged me. It was my turn to pick a word.

Eight letters.

Red chose E.

Two of those.

Yellow chose R.

Three of those and now the end of the word was there.

"Cheaters." I glared at them. "You're in cahoots."

Cahoots was a great word too. Maybe I should've picked that one.

Brown guessed the word was *murderer* and laughed when I called it names.

"You can pretend all you want, but I'm not going anywhere. I'm inside you, girl. You have my blood, and you can't get away from it."

I shook my head and picked another word. Red said I couldn't take another turn. I told him to fuck himself and went anyway.

"You're going to destroy everyone you love. Kill them like I killed the ones I loved. That's why I didn't kill you, you know. Because I didn't love you. I loved your mother, and I killed her."

My head whipped around, and I pointed at him. "No. You don't get to say that."

I saw the knife, and then he raised it, ran toward me, and I couldn't run away. I raised my arms over my head and screamed. And screamed. And screamed.

The door opened, and I kept screaming because he was cutting me, sawing into me, breaking me.

Then a pinch and the colors came back again, soft and warm. Comforting.

I stopped screaming.

FIVE

TIME WAS PASSING TOO FAST, AND I HADN'T DONE anything yet. Sometimes there was food, and sometimes I ate it. Nothing fancy. Sometimes cereal or toast. Sometimes peanut butter and fruit. Once there was some soup, but the peas in it sang, and I couldn't eat them. It was my favorite song. I sang with them for a while, but I sang quietly because if I wasn't quiet, the angry man came and told me that things would be bad if I made any noise.

I didn't like the angry man. The scrawny man was better, not because he was nice, but because he didn't say anything at all. Then, someone new came in. He was younger than the other two. Close to my age, maybe a year or two, younger. He was different, and not just because of his age. His face was soft, like he hadn't seen or done as much as the other two. The thing that really stood out, though, was the expression in his dark eyes when he looked at me.

Pity.

I never thought I'd be happy to see someone pity me. I could use that, I realized.

Looking the way I did, I doubted a seduction would have worked. But if I could play the damsel in distress, maybe I could appeal to his inner white knight. He didn't seem jaded enough to question my sincerity. If he hadn't been one of my kidnappers, I might have felt guilty.

The next time he came in, I smiled at him. Not a sexy sort of smile, but the kind that said I was grateful for the smallest kindness. His eyes caught mine, and he smiled back. A part of me wanted to move right now, but I knew I needed to wait. I needed a clear head, and for that, I needed these drugs out of my system.

Which meant I needed to convince my white knight that I was harmless and no longer needed the drugs. When he set down the plate and cup, I cowered against the wall.

"Please, don't hurt me. I promise I'll be good." To my shame, the quiver in my voice was real.

When he pulled the syringe from his pocket, I let out a whimper. That's when I saw it. The glimmer of the doubt about what he'd been told to do.

"I don't need that anymore. I won't scream. Please don't make me take it." I wrapped my arms tight around my body and shivered. "It makes me see things. Scary things. Last time, I started screaming and..." I swallowed hard before I continued, "that's when he hit me."

The young man frowned. "He hit you?"

I sniffled and nodded. I put my hand to my cheek, wincing as if it still hurt. I didn't need to fake how tender my ribs still were, only let it show on my face. I needed to be careful not to overplay my hand. If I pushed too much, I'd lose him and never get out.

"I have to give it to you. It's my job." He cast a furtive glance at the door behind him. "You don't know what they'll do to me if I don't."

I wanted to snap back that I knew damn well what they do to him because I'd been on the receiving end of one of Serge's punishments. At least he had the freedom to choose whether to stay. I couldn't say any of that, though, because I needed him on my side.

"Please," I begged. "Maybe only give me a little. If anyone notices, you can say you didn't want me to overdose. They might think you're playing it safe, but they won't be mad."

I held my breath as I watched him consider the idea. It wasn't the best possibility, but at least it was something. After a moment, he nodded.

"Alright," he said, "I'll give you half a dose. Hopefully, it'll be enough to keep away anything scary."

"Thank you," I said breathlessly. "Thank you so much."

I almost added something about how I could repay him, but I thought that might go too far. Besides, I didn't want to put ideas in his head. I'd made it this far without being raped.

I closed my eyes and held out my arm, hating how submissive the gesture felt. It was one thing to not fight. It was something else altogether to participate. And this felt a hell of a lot like participating. Tears stung my eyelids, but I didn't brush them away. I'd let him think they were tears of gratitude instead of shame.

"What's your name?" I asked. For a moment, I didn't think he'd answer me. There was power in a name.

"Yerik."

"Thank you, Yerik. I'm Rona."

I knew he knew my name, but one of the basics to surviving kidnapping or hostage situation was consistent reminders of humanity. I couldn't become just another nameless, faceless woman. I needed to have a name.

As he stood, I looked up at him with pleading on my face, and said, "Will you come again, Yerik? Please. I'd rather it be you."

His cheeks flushed, and after a moment, he nodded. We stayed like that for several seconds before he turned and walked away, leaving me with a clear enough mind to start thinking about escape.

I had to make sure no one else knew what Yerik had done for me. I wasn't going soft. When I got out of there, I'd see that the FBI offered him a deal to flip on the others, but that was all he was getting from my gratitude. No matter how young or easily manipulated he was, Yerik was still involved in holding me captive.

I talked, doing my best to match the cadence and volume that I'd had the previous few days when I'd been on full doses of the drugs. I didn't really think about what I was saying, letting random bits of what sounded like half of a conversation come out all on its own. It didn't matter if any of it was based on real events or feelings. The privacy of my personal life wasn't really my top concern now.

My brain wasn't buzzing as fast as usual, but this wasn't exactly a complex escape plan. It would come down to timing and sheer physicality. I would need to catch someone off-guard enough that I could not only get to the door but through the door. I couldn't risk someone grabbing me just as I got outside the room.

That was another problem. I didn't know what was outside. I could find stairs and another door with more mysteries behind it. It could be a house or a warehouse, in any sort of neighborhood. Once I made it out of this hateful room, I needed to get out of the building without being caught, then hope that I recognized where I was. I'd been in Fort Collins long enough to know my way around for the most part, but there were still parts of the city where I'd be lost. Granted, being lost was better than my current situation.

The odds were in my favor that even if I didn't know where I was, I could find someone to lend me their phone. Then again, I had to consider the danger to which I'd be exposing anyone who helped me. The last thing I wanted was someone getting hurt. Or worse.

Size wise, it made more sense for me to go after the scrawny guy. But I thought that Yerik would hesitate, and that might give me the edge I needed to get free. I would've liked to wait a little more, but I knew I couldn't count on Yerik to come back more than once. The next time the door opened, if it was him, I had to go.

As far as I could tell, my cell didn't have any cameras, but I still took a risk when I pushed myself to my feet. I'd gotten rid of the tape around my ankles at some point. Fortunately, they assumed I was too far out of it to need them tied again.

I took it slow, making it look like I was wandering, chasing after things only I could see. My legs could barely hold at first, and it frightened me how weak I'd gotten in such a short time. Still, I didn't give in to the desire to fade into nothing, to just let go. There was no way in hell I was going down without a fight.

Around the room I went, slowly stretching my arms and legs, testing to see where my weaknesses were. The colors were still there, in the background, swirling and muted, but I ignored them. It was easier to do while I was moving, and it gave me hope that this could actually work.

I heard the footsteps, and I told myself this was it. It was time.

I braced myself across from the door, knowing I'd need the momentum. Then the door opened, and the moment I saw Yerik's face, I moved. No overthinking, no hesitation. I caught a glimpse of surprise on his face as I shoved past him, but I didn't slow down.

The corridor was dark, but I caught a glimpse of light several feet away. I ran toward it, knowing it was my only hope. It wasn't until I grabbed the doorknob that I thought I hadn't considered what to do if the door was locked. For a sweet few seconds, as the doorknob turned under my hand, I could almost taste freedom. Then the door opened, and I hit a wall of muscle and bounced off.

Serge grabbed my arms in a bruising grip, the expression on his face promising more pain. I barely felt it over the despair that flooded me. This was it. I doubted I'd get another chance. Whatever horrors they had in store for me, I would have no choice but to face them. Still, I would not let them break me.

SIX

THE FLOOR WAS COLD, AND THEY TOOK MY COAT, BUT sometimes the colors came and kept me warm. *He* hadn't come back since I'd screamed him away, but sometimes others came.

"You're a really good agent," I told Clay. "I'm glad that no one found out about us. It was stupid for us to fuck. It wasn't anything real, and we risked your career. Don't do it again. You wait until you find someone who's worth everything, and if she's worth it, she won't ask you to risk your career. You deserve it all."

He smiled at me. That Clay smile that always made me think of the times before Anton died. Back when I still had at least some family. Before I was alone.

Like I was alone now.

Because there wasn't anyone in the room with me. Clay had left. He never stayed long. He hadn't stayed long before either.

"Anton, haven't you gotten that damn thing to work yet?"

I looked up from my seat in the corner as a tall pretty-boy came swaggering into the loft like he owned it. Unruly dark hair and a pair of intelligent blue-gray eyes. If he hadn't walked right over to the fridge and grabbed a beer like he had every right to go rooting around in the kitchen, I might have thought he was attractive.

Okay, I wasn't blind. He was hot. Younger than Uncle Anton, but older than my seventeen years.

"Want to grab me a beer too?" I asked as I set aside my book.

He looked down, surprised to see me. "You don't look old enough to drink."

I raised an eyebrow. "I believe it's legal as long as I'm at home and it's been given to me by my guardian."

"I'm not your guardian," he countered.

"You walked into my home acting like you live here, so I was confused."

He stared at me for a moment, then laughed. "I'm Clay Kurth." He held out a hand, and I shook it. "I met your uncle at the courthouse a couple weeks ago."

"You're the FBI agent who helped him carry that old turntable up here." I gestured to the hunk of junk in the corner where Uncle Anton had spent his spare time lately.

"I am," Clay said. "He was bound and determined to get that thing up here. I thought he was nuts."

"I'm not the one who went undercover in Crazy Tony's crew to make a racketeering case," Anton said mildly.

I gave Clay another look. Anton made sure I stayed away from the more unsavory parts of Hell's Kitchen, but I would've had to be deaf to not know who Crazy Tony was.

This FBI agent was either incredibly brave...or an idiot. I was leaning toward the latter.

Clay had come around a few more times before Anton died, and after that, he'd kept an eye on me, eventually recruiting me to the FBI. I doubted Uncle Anton would've approved of the two of us sleeping together, but I knew he would've been glad to know that I had someone like Clay at my back.

Back.

Back.

My back was against the wall. It was cold. My colors had gone away again. Food would come soon, and with it, the needle and the colors. I wouldn't feel the cold or the fear that wanted to sneak in when those thoughts crept in again. The thoughts that asked where I was and what was going to happen to me.

"Did he hurt you again?"

Jalen looked worried as he crouched next to me. I slowly shook my head as he brushed his finger down my cheek.

"As long as I don't scream, he doesn't hurt me," I said. "And I don't need to scream when you and Clay are here to protect me." I grabbed his hand. "Don't be mad about Clay. He's my friend."

"I know," Jalen said. He brought my hand to his mouth and kissed my knuckles. "He's a good guy."

I nodded emphatically, then closed my eyes for a moment. Too much moving made me dizzy. I kept talking though. I liked talking to Jalen.

"He is a good guy. I really want you two to get along."

"We do."

I opened my eyes to see Clay sitting next to Jalen. I didn't know which one had spoken, but it didn't matter because they were both holding my hand now.

"You're going to find me," I said as I stretched out on the floor. My room stunk, and I knew I was almost as dirty as the floor, but Clay and Jalen didn't seem to mind. "Will you keep me warm until the colors come?"

Clay laid down behind me and wrapped his arms around me. Jalen laid in front of me, his arms sliding between Clay's waist and mine. He rested his forehead on mine, and the heat from their bodies seeped into me.

"Are you looking for me?" I whispered. I didn't want Serge or his friends to overhear. If they knew Jalen and Clay were coming for me, they might move me, and then no one would ever find me.

"Of course," Jalen said, brushing his lips against my cheek, my mouth. "I'll never stop looking for you. I promise."

"What about the baby?"

"Don't worry about that," he said, his hand sliding under my shirt. His fingers traced my scar. "Elise was lying. There's no baby. The only person I want a baby with is you."

"I don't think I'll be a good parent," I admitted. "I don't know what it's like to have good parents."

"Yes, you do," Clay said quietly. "Before your dad's accident, you had good parents. Your mom was always amazing. Anton wasn't perfect, but he was good too. You know how to love."

"Dad said he didn't love me."

"Shh." Jalen smoothed down my matted hair. "You can remember what it was like before the accident. You know he loved you. Just remember."

Another crack of lightning was close enough for me to

hear it. Thunder rumbled almost immediately, rattling the pictures on my walls. My heart beat rapidly against my ribs, and I slid out of bed. It was too much to deal with alone. I was a big girl, but even big girls were scared sometimes. Daddy told me that, and Daddy didn't lie.

I ran across the hall into their room, right up to Daddy's side of the bed. I tugged on the blanket. "Daddy."

He snored, but right now I didn't think it was funny how he sounded like a sleeping bear. I didn't want to laugh. I wanted him to wake up.

"Daddy." I grabbed his hand this time and pulled on it. "Daddy wake up!"

He blinked at me. "Rona? Are you okay, little ladybug?"

I shook my head. "I'm scared."

He didn't ask me why I was scared or what had scared me. He just leaned over and picked me up, rolling us both over so that I was between him and Mommy. That was the safest place to be. No one could get me when I was here. Mommy and Daddy protected me. Kept me safe. They'd never let anyone hurt me.

I jerked awake, my befuddled brain unsure when I'd fallen asleep. Clay and Jalen were gone, and a part of me recognized the fact that they'd never been here to begin with. Someone had been though, because I had new food and water, and a familiar ache in my arm from another injection.

I should be worried about that. Were they using the same syringe? Had they used it on anyone else? What was in it? Was I going to come out of this addicted or damaged? I'd made it through nearly being cut in half without getting addicted to painkillers. I couldn't let this ruin me.

Clarity of thought didn't last long, not with another dose

of drugs making its way through my system. Before I could get worked up enough to attempt anything remotely close to an escape plan, my limbs began to feel heavy, and the colors came back.

"If you can't think, you'll never be able to get out of here." Jalen nudged my plate with his toe. "You've been here for too long already."

I ate my toast and a pear. I didn't tell him that I couldn't have been here too long because I didn't know how much time had passed. Maybe Serge was feeding me every few hours to make me think I'd been gone for days, but it was only Saturday.

"You were in the FBI," Jalen said. "You know the chances of finding a kidnap victim goes down with every passing hour."

"I wasn't in the FBI," I said. The drugs blunted my tongue, and the words came out slurred. "I got kicked out for lying."

"Why did you lie?" Clay asked as he appeared next to Jalen. "You had to know the FBI would figure it out."

"Because it's easier to get kicked out than it is to fail," Jalen answered the question when I could only stare. "Why do you think she dated you? Friends with benefits but with plenty of reasons to cut and run if things got too tough, too emotional. You were practically her supervisor."

"No, he wasn't," I cut in, glaring at Jalen. "It wasn't like that. Clay and I had fun, but that's all it was."

"That's all it is with you too," Clay said with a smarmy sort of grin. The kind I'd never seen on his face before. "I'll bet she's already given you a reason why she needs some 'space' or 'time.'"

Jalen's expression shifted, as if something about Clay's words made him think. "She did say she needed some time to think about things."

"To think about your *wife* being *pregnant* with your *child!*" I barely managed to keep from shouting. "Anyone would need some time to process that."

Clay shook his head. "She's just looking for excuses to get out."

"I'm not," I hissed at him. "I don't want to 'get out' of this thing with Jalen."

"'This thing'?" he echoed. "Is that all we are to each other?"

"Go away!" I clapped my hands over my mouth as soon as I shouted the words.

I stared at the door as sickly yellows and greens swirled around my head. It'd only been two words, and I hadn't screamed them. Maybe no one heard. Maybe they'd forgive me because I'd been so good. I hadn't tried to run away or fight since years ago. Or hours. I still didn't know.

My churning stomach calmed as the door stayed shut. That was good. I didn't want to throw up. I'd already drunk all my water, and I didn't have a place to rinse my mouth out. No bathroom at all. Not even a bucket.

I wrinkled my nose. I didn't want to think about that.

"Of course you don't," Clay said. "You never want to think about the unpleasant things. It's easier to just pretend everything's fine and then run away when it gets hard."

"I didn't run away."

"You sabotaged your FBI career before it even really began," he pointed out. "You kept your shirt on when we had sex because you didn't want me to see your scar, and I knew the second I pushed you on the subject, you'd be out the door."

I wanted to tell him that wasn't true, but I knew it was. I pressed my face against my knees and covered my ears. I didn't want to talk to Clay anymore. I just wanted to drift on the colors and not have to think.

"I love this time of day," Jalen said as he slipped his arm around my shoulders and pulled me tight against his side. "Not quite afternoon, not quite evening. It's the sort of time that makes me feel like anything's possible."

"Anything is possible," I reminded him. I ran my hand over my stomach, smoothing down the soft cotton of my maternity shirt.

It seemed like I'd gone from a slight little bump to showing almost overnight. In no time at all, our little one would be here, and we hadn't even begun discussing names.

"What do you think of the name Dana?" I asked. "If it's a girl, I think we should name her Dana, after my mother."

"You want to name our child after a woman who was murdered?" Jalen asked.

I pretended his comment didn't hurt. "She didn't do anything wrong."

"She should have left your father the first time she saw that the accident changed him."

I wanted to argue with him, but I'd said those words too. The first year after...it happened, I'd blamed her. I'd screamed those words at Anton dozens of times those first couple years. The bitterness would have eaten away at me if Anton hadn't told me that it was okay to be angry. That adults made mistakes, that they didn't know everything. He told me that if my mother had known what my father would do, she would've made different choices.

I still struggled with anger for years after that, but the bitterness was gone. I could love my mom again even as I acknowledged how different things would have been if she'd made different choices.

I mustered a smile for Jalen and tried again. "What do you think?"

He shrugged. "Let's just call her Denise."

I frowned. "That's the name of your other daughter."

"I know," he said. "It'll just make things easier for me, not having to remember two names."

A cramp in my leg yanked me out of the nightmare, but it was too late. Tears streamed down my cheeks, and I scrubbed at them, knowing I was just making things worse. I was filthy, disgusting, and it was no wonder that no one had come for me. No one wanted me badly enough to come.

Dimly, I wondered if the drugs they were giving me were affecting my mood as much as my thoughts, but I couldn't hold on to the idea long enough to really think about it. Instead, my mind latched onto something else, and I gratefully followed.

SEVEN

Someone had cleaned out my cell. Not like scrubbed down clean, but enough so that the stench wasn't overwhelming. I doubted it was because of me. I'd heard scrawny guy gag the last time he'd come in to give me my food and my shot. He was the only one I recognized besides Serge, but I wasn't sure anyone else had come in at all. I was aware enough of my situation to know that I couldn't completely trust anything I saw or heard.

At times like these, it wasn't hard to remember. Red and I were having a great conversation about pizza toppings, but even as I laughed, a part of me knew that I was alone, talking to colors and people who weren't even there.

But it didn't stop me. My only other option was to try to fight the drugs, but it was a fight I couldn't win. Not without losing my mind. Serge had turned the lights off the last two times between meals, and I'd felt panic at the edges of my mind. Then Jalen had appeared, and we'd talked until I'd fallen asleep.

I couldn't do this much longer. I wasn't strong enough. I'd never been strong enough. It was a good thing I hadn't made it into the FBI because I would've been a shit agent.

"No, you would've been great."

I rolled my eyes and flicked Clay off.

"C'mon, Rona. Don't you remember when I came to recruit you?"

I did.

"You look like shit, kid. When's the last time you slept?"

I looked up from my abnormal psychology textbook to see a familiar face standing over me. "Clay? What are you doing here?"

He swung one long leg over the chair across from me and sat down without asking for permission. He crossed his arms and leaned on the table. "I told you that I'd be checking in on you from time to time."

I shrugged. He'd made the promise at Uncle Anton's funeral a couple months ago, but I hadn't expected it to last long. I wasn't anything to Clay. His friend's niece. Some kid who was always underfoot and mouthing off to him.

"You didn't think I'd do it." He sounded more amused than annoyed. "No matter. I've been keeping an eye on you even when I'm not here."

"That's not at all creepy."

He laughed, showing those straight, white teeth of his. "When you started at Columbia, Anton suggested to me the possibility that you might be a good candidate for the FBI."

It was my turn to laugh, and I stretched my arms over my head as I did so. It'd been a while since I'd moved, and my muscles were stiff. "Are you trying to recruit me?"

"Anton said you intended to maybe go into criminal

psychology and become a detective, but I think you'd make an excellent intelligence analyst with the FBI."

An intelligence analyst with the FBI. That hadn't been on my radar before, but now that he'd mentioned it, I could see it. Still, a part of me was wary.

"Why?" I leaned back in my chair. "What makes you think I'd be any good in the FBI?"

Clay's eyes narrowed, and he gave me a searching look, waiting nearly a full minute before answering my question. "I don't know a lot about what brought you and Anton together, but I know how passionate you are about justice. After what happened to your uncle, I think you're even more driven to find ways to right wrongs."

"Okay, but why the FBI? Why not at the local level?"

He smiled again. "Because you're meant for greater things than New York City Homicide."

"Greater things," I muttered as I rolled over to face the wall. "Right. I'm meant for big things. Like being a PI in Colorado."

"You saved Meka and other girls from being sold as sex slaves." Jalen's voice came from behind me. "And you helped stop a human trafficking ring that provided sweatshop labor. I'd say that isn't bad for a PI."

I shrugged. "Jenna did most of the work."

"We both know that's bullshit," he countered. "Jenna would say the same. Didn't she hire you to find her siblings rather than doing it herself?"

"Not the same."

The door opened, but I didn't roll over again, not even when the light came on. I squeezed my eyes shut, antici-pating the pain from my light-deprived eyes. I could find the food after he left, and he could stick me from behind as well as he could stick me facing him. He'd done it before.

"You really like to talk." It was Serge's voice, not the scrawny man. "Most people on this, they just laugh and babble. You did some of that too, but you carry on entire conversations. Who are you seeing?"

"Nobody. No one. Nobody. No one." I shook my head. He couldn't know about Jalen or Clay. If he knew, he'd stop them from coming for me.

"It doesn't matter," Serge said. "In the morning, we're going to get you cleaned up. A shower. Soap. Shampoo. Does that sound good?"

"Yes." I waited to hear what I would have to do for it. The colors whispered all sorts of nasty things, but I glared at them. I needed to hear it from him first. Besides, if he'd wanted to fuck me, he would've done it already. I wasn't so out of it that I wouldn't have noticed that.

"I'm going to lower your dosage in the morning," he continued. "Big dose tonight, little one tomorrow. But you have to be good, or my employers will be even angrier at you than they already are."

His employers. He'd talked about them before. He said that I'd pissed them off. But I didn't know who he was talking about. Every time I asked, I didn't get answers. I didn't bother asking this time. It wouldn't do any good.

"You will clean up nicely," he said. "There will be makeup for you to cover bruises. No one will bid on you if they believe you are not controllable. Some men like to break their women themselves, but all want them malleable at purchase."

Some part at the back of my brain sent off warning bells

as Serge spoke, but as soon as I heard one word, I forgot it for the next. I could barely put together the fact that I was going to get to take a shower tomorrow, let alone what it was for. It was important, but I'd have to wait until the morning to start figuring it out. Why I'd be able to figure it out in the morning, I didn't know, but something told me that I just needed to wait.

"Hold on," Jalen whispered in my ear. "Just hold on a little longer."

I wanted to tell him that I would, but the colors were too loud, their shouts drowning him out.

Tomorrow.

Tomorrow.

EIGHT

I HADN'T REALIZED HOW MUCH I'D MISSED BEING CLEAN until I stepped under the warm spray and felt the dirt slough off. I didn't even want to consider what that 'dirt' was made up of. Fortunately, Serge had made good on his promise and gave me another shot, so anything I didn't want to think about too hard, I just let slip away.

The shampoo smelled good. Clean, but without any of the extra stuff like fake-cherries. The soap was the same, and I vaguely wondered if it had been bought in bulk. I'd thought before about whether I was the only woman who'd been kept here, and the generic nature of the soap made me think that others could have gone through the same thing.

The world was still fuzzy, but when I stepped out of the shower, I felt more human than I had in days. I took my time drying off, in part because it just felt good to be clean again, but also because I needed the time alone to think. Really think. Thanks to the drugs still making their way through my system, my mind was far from as fast as I was accustomed to, but it was much better than it had been since I arrived. Even better than when I'd made my ill-fated escape attempt.

The next one wouldn't be an attempt.

Suddenly, I remembered what Serge said last night. If, indeed, it had been last night. I still didn't know what day it was. I could only hope that my friends hadn't given up on me. Because I had friends, and the realization startled me. It wasn't only Clay and Jalen who would've missed me by now. I had Jenna and Rylan too. Because Jenna wasn't only a client, she was a friend as well. And if I really thought about it, Jenna was as likely to find me as anyone. Maybe more because she didn't always feel the need to follow the law.

It wasn't until the guard knocked on the door that I remembered there was a reason for me cleaning up, and I'd gotten distracted. Serge had told me that his employers had a plan for me. If only I could remember what that was. The memory hovered at the back of my mind, just out of reach.

"Let's go."

Shit. It was Yerik. I hadn't seen him since I'd almost escaped. I hadn't thought about him since then either but considering all the shit I'd had pumped into me, that wasn't a surprise. Now, however, I realized how shocking it was that he was still alive. I wondered if perhaps he had a connection to Serge or one of the employers, but a part of me hoped it was because Serge figured it was better to punish for a failure and give someone the chance to improve rather than kill them. I didn't want Yerik's blood on my hands, especially not when there was always a chance he could be rehabilitated.

"You've got, ten seconds before I come in there, naked or not."

Right. Focus.

I reached for the clothes on the counter without really seeing them. They were clean, and that was all I cared about...until I pulled up the panties and realized that they were basically a sheer lace thong. And I hadn't been given a bra.

What the fuck?

I picked up the dress, and that was when all the pieces came together, though I wished to hell that they hadn't.

Auction.

That was what Serge had said.

I was being taken to an auction.

Based on the low cut, high hem, and clingy material, it was easy to figure out exactly why people would be bidding on me. I hated the idea of going along with it even for one second, but I pulled the dress over my head. It was a deep, rich blue. The sort of dress that didn't require a bra, not that I'd been given one. My nipples pebbled as the soft material slid over my body, and if I'd been wearing it for Jalen, I would've enjoyed every sensual moment.

The door didn't have a lock and opened easily. Yerik looked pissed, but he didn't glare at me. He didn't even look at me. From the bruises on his face, it wasn't hard to understand why.

"Let's go." He held out a hand, but I knew it wasn't for me to take. No matter how I looked in this dress, he didn't want to touch me.

Maybe it made me a bad person, but I didn't feel guilty about it at all. He was alive and not in the hospital. Even if he'd never been involved in one of these situations before, he wasn't stupid. He knew what was going to be done to me tonight if I didn't get away.

I could've used his unwillingness to touch me, but it was too risky. I'd humiliated him. Right now, he was either going the shame route, or he was keeping a leash on his anger because he knew he'd get in even more trouble if he marked me before the auction. If I pushed him too far, he might forget about self-preservation and lash out.

That would be bad for both of us.

I stepped out of the bathroom and saw a pair of flats off to the side. I was a bit surprised. A dress like this really went with heels. Then I realized that they probably thought that heels could be a weapon.

They were right.

I put on the shoes and followed Yerik meekly as he led me down a corridor. The motion after so much lack of motion spun my mind too fast for me to keep up, but I didn't bother trying to memorize it all. I didn't plan on coming back here.

The cold burst of air registered before I even understood that I was outside. I caught the sharp smell of snow, then felt it on my face, but only for a few seconds before I was nudged into the back of a car and a door shut behind me.

The windows were heavily tinted, to the point where I couldn't really see out, but I supposed that was the point. Still, I strained to find something familiar, some landmark that would tell me where I was.

"Don't bother," Serge said easily. "You can't get out of the car unless I unlock the doors, and I won't be doing that until we reach our destination."

"The auction," I said.

He nodded. "My employers are convinced that you'll fetch a high price. Perhaps our highest. I don't agree."

I didn't bother to attempt a response, and I doubted he

expected one. He assumed I was going to try to escape again, and I would do my best to not disappoint him, but not now. He'd helped me with that comment. If I hadn't known that only he could unlock the doors, I might've wasted time planning to get out and run before we got to wherever we were going. Now, I focused my energy on something else.

I RESISTED the urge to scrub my palms on my thighs like I would have if I'd been wearing jeans. I couldn't give anything away. Serge and the scrawny guy flanked me as we walked, making no illusions about which of the...properties was the most valuable. There were others behind me, other girls I could hear whispering in frightened breaths of sound. I hadn't seen how many when Yerik had unloaded them from the van that had pulled into the parking garage behind us, but the sheer fact that it was more than just me told me that whatever was going on here was a hell of a lot bigger than I'd originally anticipated.

Once I got out, I'd get ahold of Clay, and he would send men in to rescue the rest. Jenna would help him find every one of these sons of bitches who hid behind the two-way mirrors and in the shadows.

"A word of warning," Serge said as he grabbed my arm. "Don't. Be. Stupid."

I ignored him. I was going to be stupid very shortly, and his warning wouldn't change that.

We made another turn, and I finally caught a glimpse of what I'd been looking for from the moment we stepped inside.

Red light.

Exit.

The people involved here might be heartless bastards who had no problems with buying and selling human beings for all sorts of depravities, but they weren't stupid enough to put themselves into a building without fire exits.

The moment Serge's grip loosened, I yanked away...hard. As I'd hoped, it made my stumble into the scrawny man look unintentional. A move that threw him off balance and gave me my one chance.

I ran out of the flats, cursing the way the dress hindered my movements, but not daring to hesitate. It was going to be cold, and it wouldn't feel pleasant on my feet, but I'd take ice over this any day. I expected shouts behind me, a flurry of activity, but the only sounds I heard over the racing of my pulse were the exclamations of the other women and fists against flesh to turn those cries into ones of pain.

My hands hit the bar on the fire door, and the gust of cold nearly took my breath away. I hadn't realized how overheated I'd gotten until a full breath pierced my lungs like icicles. My feet slapped the wet blacktop, and I ran blindly, searching for something familiar, for someone, anyone, who would take me to the police.

An open door. Warmth. Strength. Safety. I'd be at a hospital soon, getting my system flushed, wounds tended. I'd be home by tomorrow. Or better yet, I'd be in bed with Jalen, sleeping in his arms.

Except none of that happened.

Oh, I tried to run, and I made it to the fire exit. But when I hit the bar, I bounced back, my feet tangling together. Strong arms caught me, but they weren't the ones I wanted.

These were hard steel, confining, bruising. They pulled me against a granite chest.

"I told you not to do anything stupid," Serge said in my ear.

I screamed, kicking my feet up and throwing myself back against him. He squeezed me harder, muttering curses as he fought to hold me still. I didn't stop, twisting and using as much of my body weight as I could, anything that could get me out of his grip and through that damn door. Except I couldn't breathe, and screaming had emptied my lungs until spots exploded in front of my eyes.

And then I felt it. The all-too-familiar sting of the needle, then the rush of drugs making my head spin.

My body went slack, and I forgot what I was doing. Forgot why it hurt so much to breathe. Two blows to the stomach had me retching, but the pain was muddled as the colors came flooding back, dancing around as someone pulled me to my feet and ordered me to walk again.

Time slipped and swirled, and then I was standing on a stage, staring stupidly into a blinding light as I tried to remember why I should care about being here like this. Men's voices came from behind the lights, but their voices blended together, making it impossible for me to understand what anyone was saying.

Someone listed numbers that kept growing higher and higher until, finally, I made out a single word.

Sold.

I'd been sold.

I swayed, trying to remember why those words sent a shiver of fear down my spine, but it was all I could do to stay on my own two feet.

Iron fingers dug into my arm, and I heard a bark of displeasure. The grip lessened, and I frowned but didn't pull away. My muscles felt rubbery, weak, and I could barely feel my feet. I saw another girl shuffle past as I was pushed out of the way, and I felt a dull throb of helpless anger that I couldn't do anything to change her fate any more than I could my own.

"Just keep walking." A man's voice came from next to me. "Just keep walking."

I nodded and concentrated on putting one foot in front of the other.

NINE

THAT BEEPING WAS DAMN ANNOYING, BUT I HAD AN IDEA that it was important. I wasn't yet sure why, but it'd come to me eventually, I was sure.

For now, I was content with my change in circumstances. I had an inkling that they were supposed to somehow be worse than they had been, but I didn't have the energy to question it. Instead, I stared up at the ceiling and enjoyed the fact that I was warm and laying on something much softer than the floor.

"I was hoping you'd come," I said as I heard the scrape of a chair. I didn't need to look over to know who was sitting there. I would know him anywhere.

"Rona? You're awake?"

Fingers closed around mine, but I still didn't look. With everything that had happened, a part of me knew that my brain wasn't quite all back to normal, but I was okay with talking to hallucinations. On some level, I was aware that I'd been doing it since I was drugged the first time. It was how I'd coped in my basement cell, and it would get me through whatever came next.

"I'm not sure," I answered slowly.

"Not sure what, baby?" His voice was soft, and it made me smile.

"Not sure if I'm awake." I turned my head finally, grimacing at the ache in my muscles, but it was worth it to see his face again.

Even though he looked rough. Stubble, dark shadows under his eyes, wrinkled clothes.

My hallucinations were getting even more detailed than they had been before.

"Why's that?" he asked as he smoothed his free hand over my forehead.

"Colors have been talking," I whispered.

His eyes widened slightly. "Really? And what have they been saying?"

I shrugged. "All sorts of things. We played games, but sometimes they cheated. You and Clay wouldn't play with me. All you ever wanted to do was talk."

"We talked." He made it a statement rather than a question.

I rolled my eyes. "Of course we talked. All the time. You and me and Clay."

There was a pause, and for a moment, something real flickered across his eyes. But it couldn't be real because I hadn't escaped. Serge had caught me, and I'd been sold. I still remembered that. So even if I was somewhere warm and laying on something soft, it was only because the person who bought me wanted me healthy so that he could hurt me however he wanted.

"I liked that you were getting along," I admitted. "It was nice, being able to talk to both of you together."

He got a thoughtful look on his face, and he rubbed his thumb over my knuckles. "Clay really means a lot to you, huh?"

I nodded. "He's family." I scowled. "Not exactly, since that'd be gross, but you know what I mean. Clay was there, even after Anton died."

"You need him."

I shook my head. I didn't like the way he sounded. Sad. Resolved.

"He's a friend. That's all."

"And what am I?"

If he hadn't been an illusion inside my head, I would've thought he was talking to himself, but since he wasn't real, I answered him with the simplest, most straightforward response I could give. "You're everything."

TEN

I sucked in a breath and jolted upright, eyes wide, and my mind brutally, and *finally*, clear.

I was awake. Really, truly awake, and information inundated every one of my senses in an almost overwhelming flood.

I was in a hospital. The beeping that had made its way into my subconscious made sense now. Based on the quality of the sheets I felt under my palms and the fact that I appeared to be in a private room. I had an IV in my hand and one of those clip things on my finger. I was still sore, which meant I hadn't been out that long, though I didn't know specifics about when or where I was.

Or if I was safe.

A private room in a hospital didn't necessarily mean that I'd been somehow rescued. Until I saw proof that I wasn't still a prisoner, I needed to keep my wits about me. Who knew–

"Rona, thank God you're awake."

I turned toward the door, half hoping that I was mistaken and that I would see Jalen. Instead, I saw the person I second most wanted to see. "Clay."

He crossed the room quickly, the relief obvious on his face. "I was so worried."

I was glad to see him, I really was, but I couldn't help but feel a little disappointed that Jalen wasn't there. I wasn't surprised though. He had a baby to think of now, after all. I refused to be sad. Clay was there, and I was alive. Not only alive, but free.

He crushed me in a hug, then cursed when I made a pained sound. He immediately released me but didn't move away. He wrapped his hands around mine, mindful of the IV.

"What day is it?" I asked.

"Sunday," he said, his eyes moving over my body, as if he was reassuring himself that I was real.

I knew the feeling.

"I've only been gone for three days?" I frowned. "It seemed like more."

He shook his head. "You were missing for eight days, and you've been here since Friday night."

A memory battled through the drug-induced fog of my time away.

"What about the others?" I looked around even though I'd already seen that I was alone.

"The others?"

"The other girls," I said impatiently. "Are they okay?" More memories prompted more questions. "What about Serge and Yerik and the other men who took me? And those bastards at the auction? Did you get them all?"

The baffled expression on Clay's face was the first indication that something was off.

"Clay," I spoke slowly, unsure if I really wanted an answer, "what happened while I was gone?"

He sat down in a chair I hadn't noticed before, pulling it closer so he could reach for my hand again. I was tempted to pull away until he explained whatever it was that had him looking like he'd been hit by a two-by-four, but I needed the comfort of a familiar touch.

"I tried calling you on Friday morning to ask you about one of the cases you were looking into for Jenna." He looked down at our hands. "When you didn't answer, I texted you. By noon, I knew something was wrong, so I went to see Jalen at work."

I braced myself for whatever Jalen had told Clay about the last time we'd been together.

"He wasn't there."

A flash of pain went through me. Jalen had probably been busy with Elise. Doctor appointments. Shopping for baby stuff. Working out living arrangements.

"I finally got one of his employees to tell me where he was." Clay's eyes flicked up to my face, then fell again. "He was with Jenna."

I frowned. Jenna?

"I went over and found the two of them in front of computers, looking like they hadn't slept in a day and a half. They hadn't been able to get ahold of you either."

They'd noticed. All three of them had noticed that I was gone. Even as busy as they were with their families and jobs, they'd missed me. A lump formed in my throat.

"Jalen and I went to the police to file a missing person's

report," Clay continued. "I wanted something official in the system when I petitioned the FBI to let me use our resources to find you, but they wouldn't help. First, they said that it hadn't been long enough. Then it was because of what happened between you and Jalen the last time he saw you. He said you two hadn't broken up, but they clearly didn't believe it."

Based on his tone, I suspected that the cops weren't the only ones who hadn't believed it. I didn't press it though. I wanted to know more and getting us off-track by talking about my relationship with Jalen wouldn't accomplish anything.

"Then they asked if you had a history of leaving and not telling anyone, of cutting off contact without warning." His eyes finally met mine. "I had no way of knowing if this time was different than when you bolted from Virginia."

I kept my lips pressed together to keep me from saying something that I'd regret. He knew damn well this wasn't the same. Jalen and I were in a relationship. I never would've just left without talking to him at least. In Virginia, I'd been lost, reeling from being expelled, my future suddenly empty. Here, I had a business. A home. Friends. Without the FBI, the only thing I'd had in Virginia had been him. And what we'd had never would have been enough to hold me, no matter how much he wanted to believe it.

"What happened next?" I asked, my voice as stiff as I felt. I rubbed my fingers, both of us pretending that was the reason I'd pulled my hand away.

"I went to the office and made some calls," he said. "I spoke to the warden in Indiana and had your father's corre- spondence checked. I got a list of his visitors, the calls he'd made and received. I had the warden talk to other prisoners and to your father."

My dad? My forehead furrowed as I frowned. He was a lot of things, many of them horrible, but he wasn't a human trafficker. He'd tried to kill me, sure, but he'd never *sell* me. And he sure as hell didn't have the resources to pull off something like that auction, even if he'd suddenly decided to go into business.

"While I was doing that, Jenna was digging on her own and Jalen was out on foot," Clay continued. "He retraced your steps over and over, starting where he'd last seen you and going through all sorts of possibilities. Saturday afternoon, he called me, but I was busy and didn't pick up. That evening, I got a call from Jenna, but I didn't answer that one either. I figured if anyone was going to find you, it would be me."

Clay hadn't found me. The realization stunned me. I'd been certain that my rescue had been the result of an FBI raid he'd led. Now, I had no idea what'd happened.

He ran his hand through his hair, then rubbed his jaw. "I kept ignoring them, sometimes intentionally, sometimes not. If I'd only listened..." He shook his head, his expression haunted. "The reason they'd been calling me was that Jalen had found your phone in a ditch near his house, and Jenna had dug deep into activity around your father. The two of them were convinced that you'd been taken by someone not connected to your dad, but when they finally talked to me on Monday morning, I told them they were wrong."

Monday morning. Jalen and Jenna had known by Monday morning that I'd been kidnapped, but I'd spent four more days in my cell. Even though I hadn't yet heard the end of the story, I couldn't help but blame Clay.

"I didn't talk to them again until Friday night when Jenna called to tell me you were here." He stretched out his hand again but stopped short of touching me. "That's when I found out what Jalen had done."

My blood ran cold at the way Clay delivered that single statement. "What did he do?" The question barely made it past my numb lips.

"Jenna monitors the dark web for any chatter about human trafficking. Sometime on Wednesday, she heard about an auction in Wellington."

I knew the name and that it was about twenty minutes north of Fort Collins. My knowledge of it ended there.

"She said her gut told her to check it out, and when she did, she found a...catalog of people for sale. Male and female, all under the age of twenty-five. She recognized a couple of them as college students who'd been reported missing over the last few months."

My stomach lurched, and I twisted my fingers together, but I didn't ask him to stop.

"It's my fault," Clay said. "She tried to tell me, but I ignored her. She called Raymond, but I'd told him that I needed his help to find you, and Jenna was on the wrong track. She tried to do things the right way, but I was too stubborn and arrogant to listen. Jalen listened though."

The memory hit me then, clearer than the experience itself had been.

A familiar scent crept through the odors of fear and pain. A familiar arm wrapped around my waist, and a familiar voice spoke.

"*Just keep walking.*"

I knew that voice, that smell. I'd been dreaming about them, praying that I'd find them again. Now, he was here with me, and I didn't want to believe it.

"*Just keep walking.*"

"What did you let him do?" I whispered.

"I didn't *let* Jalen do anything," Clay said. He hesitated, then added, "But I didn't listen to him and Jenna either."

"Clay."

"He went undercover at the auction and bought you."

Everything stopped with that sentence. "He did *what*?"

Clay repeated his statement, but it didn't make it any less bizarre. I now knew that Jalen had been the one who'd saved me, the one who'd taken me from the auction and brought me to the hospital, but it wasn't until that exact moment that I understood *how* he'd done it. He hadn't worked with the FBI to take down a trafficking ring. He hadn't made sure that trained agents had his back while he did something insanely stupid.

He'd pretended to be one of those sleazy assholes and *bought* me.

Oh *hell* no.

ELEVEN

Clay left not too long after he got a complete statement from me about what had happened. Because of Jalen, he'd already known about the other people being sold, but Jalen hadn't been able to give him the names of any of the sellers, and he'd only had the vaguest descriptions. With what I'd given Clay, he had enough to start looking through known traffickers, and once I'd assured him that I was fine by myself, he left.

I let my mind drift aimlessly as I flipped through the television channels. I'd lost more than a week, and it was going to take some time to absorb that. Nurses and doctors came at random intervals, checking machines and poking and prodding me. I let them do their jobs, answering their questions when asked and being quiet when they didn't. They didn't ask about what I'd been through, not beyond the medical things that they needed to know.

It wasn't until a different trio of people showed up in my doorway that I perked up.

"Hey, you came!"

Jenna rolled those pale gray eyes of hers, but I knew that her casual attitude was for show. She crossed to my bed and awkwardly patted my shoulder. Knowing what I did about her past, the pat was just as good as a hug.

"I hear I have you to thank for finding me," I said.

She shrugged as Rylan came over to her side. "I've gotten used to you."

I laughed, and it felt better than I remembered. "Thank you." The sound died in my throat as Jalen came up to the other side of my bed. "Hi."

He offered me a small smile, but it didn't reach his eyes. "Hi."

After a moment of uncomfortable silence, Rylan spoke, "Have the doctors said when you'll be released?"

"Tomorrow," I said. "I would have preferred to be in my own bed tonight, but they want twenty-four hours of me awake and alert before they're ready to send me home."

"Do you want me to come pick you up?" Jenna asked. "Suzette's planning on taking the kids out Christmas shopping tomorrow, and I can work here on my laptop as well as I can work at home."

"I'll take her home," Jalen said quietly.

My heart did a quick little dance, something that the beeping heart monitor shared with everyone else in the room. I turned my head, and Jalen was there, his tall, muscular body close enough to me that my pulse skittered again. Still, I couldn't let what I wanted, get in the way of what I knew.

"You don't need to do that," I said. "I can call for a car."

Jalen's grip on the bed's handrail tightened until his

knuckles turned white. "Have you forgotten what happened the last time you called for a car?"

No, I hadn't forgotten, and I didn't like the fact that he'd decided to remind me when we had a hell of a lot, more important things to discuss.

"My boyfriend paid for me at an auction run by human traffickers."

He went completely and utterly still. "Clay." The name came out like a curse.

"I think that's our cue," Rylan said to Jenna. He kissed the top of her head, then looked at me. "Whatever you need, just call, night or day."

"I will," I promised. I looked at Jenna. "Are you working with Agent Matthews on the case?"

She glanced at Jalen, then Rylan. "Why don't we wait until you're discharged to talk about that?"

I narrowed my eyes, and she raised her eyebrows, crossing her arms as she stared back. Dammit. I nodded once, and she gave me a quick smile before she and Rylan left.

"You should get some rest," Jalen said. "You've been through a lot."

His concern just pissed me off, and I pointed my finger at him. "You shouldn't even be here."

His eyes widened in surprise. "I saved your life."

"Yeah, and you could've gotten caught and left your kid without a father."

A muscle in his jaw jumped as he clenched it. "We don't need to talk about this right now. You should–"

"Don't tell me to rest," I snapped. "I've been talking to you for more than a week without you actually being there.

Now, I want a conversation that doesn't come out of my own damn head."

To my surprise, he flushed. It took a moment, and then I realized what had happened.

"We already talked once, didn't we?" I asked, heat flooding my face. "And you asked me what you were to me."

"You said I was everything." Jalen's voice was hoarse. "Rona–"

"You should be with your wife," I said quietly.

"We both know that Elise isn't my wife," he countered. "Not in any way but semantics."

"All right," I conceded. "She might not be your wife, but she is the mother of your child."

"I don't know that," he said as he reached down to take my hand. "I don't even know if she's pregnant, let alone if the baby's mine."

He had a point. I knew he did. Just like I'd known it the day I walked out of his house. It didn't change anything.

"I don't want to be with Elise. If the baby's mine, I'll be a father, but I'm done being her husband. I was done being her husband way before that drunken night." He put his free hand on my cheek and waited until I locked eyes with him. "I don't want her, Rona. I only want *you*."

Shit. My insides warmed. "Is that why you bought me?"

He straightened, shaking his head. "You can't really be pissed about that, can you?"

"You gave money to human traffickers," I pointed out.

"I paid them to get you free," he said, his voice tight. "If I hadn't, you'd be with some fucking–" He stopped, a pained expression on his face. "I didn't want to. Understand that, please. I wanted the cops to rescue you and everyone else there. I wanted the FBI to arrest every one of those assholes. But no one would listen to me, and I was running out of time. I'm not a cop. I'm not FBI. The only thing I have going for me is money. I'd do it again."

"You left them there," I said, surprised when my voice shook. "You left all those scared kids there."

He wrapped his arms around me and pulled my head against his chest. "I tried to buy more. I swear I did. I wanted to buy them all because it was right, but also so I didn't have to see the look on your face when you realized that you made it out, but they didn't. They told me it was one purchase per customer. I offered them everything I had, Rona, I swear." He kissed the top of my head. "I would've let them bankrupt me, but they told me I could have you and leave, or they'd kill me and sell you to someone else. I couldn't stay."

I pushed my face against his chest, letting his shirt absorb my tears. I believed him, but it didn't make it hurt any less. It didn't make me feel any less like shit, any less guilty for being here, safe. I had a feeling it would be a long while before that changed.

If it ever did.

TWELVE

If I'd let him, Jalen would have stayed with me all night. He could've charmed the nurses into not enforcing visiting hours, even if he hadn't been the sort of donor to the hospital that allowed rules to be stretched for him. I'd asked him to go though. I'd told him that it'd be easier for me to rest if he wasn't there, but in truth, I couldn't come to grips with what I'd been through if he was there, filling me with all sorts of other questions and concerns.

I walked away from him that day because I needed to figure out how our lives would fit together with Elise and a baby. *If* they could fit together.

But I never had that chance. Before I could even move beyond shock, I'd been kidnapped. Now, I was stuck with two huge things I had to deal with, and no idea where to begin.

Finally, I had to admit to myself that I needed to talk to someone about all of this because I couldn't figure it out on my own. Fortunately, I knew someone who had the sort of background that would make her understand where I was coming from like no one else could.

When I woke up the next morning to discuss my release, there was only one person I wanted to call.

"You still look like shit," Jenna announced as she walked into my hospital room. "I guess that means, you're only human after all. The way Jalen went on about you all the time, I half expected you'd end up being a superhero or something. Like mild-mannered PI reveals that she is actually an alien crime fighter."

I laughed, rubbing the bandages where my IV had been. "I'm pretty sure this would be the worst secret identity ever."

Jenna smiled and raised an eyebrow. "Have you gotten the all clear yet? Because I don't know about you, but I really hate hospitals."

I stood as a nursing aid rolled a wheelchair through the door, holding onto the bedrail for support. "I'm good to go."

I was settled in the passenger seat of her car before she brought up the subject I knew had been on her mind from the moment I called her. She was more patient than I'd given her credit for.

"Are we going to talk about the elephant in the room? Or, I suppose I should say, the elephant *not* in the room." Jenna cut me a sideways glance as she pulled out of the hospital parking lot. "I specifically remember being told someone else was going to take you home today."

The bright sun reflecting from the snow hurt my eyes, and I shaded them with my hand. "Did Jalen tell you about what happened the day I was kidnapped? Why I was outside waiting for a car, I mean?"

"All he said was that the two of you had been having a discussion and you needed some space."

"I want to talk to you about everything that happened," I said, "but there's something you need to know first, and trust me, you're going to need some time to process. So if you could drop me off at home, I'll tell you what you need to know, and then I'll come by tomorrow, and we can talk."

Jenna agreed, then she drove the rest of the way without a word. It was nice to just listen to music without having to think about anything. It didn't last long, because before I knew it, we were pulling up in front of my building. I hadn't given much thought to how much it had snowed while I'd been held prisoner, but seeing the unmarked snow piled in front of my office store, it really hit me how long I'd been gone.

I knew all too well the sort of tricks time could play with a person's head. Racing along one moment, dragging the next. In some ways, it felt like I had just been here yesterday, but in others, I felt as if I'd been gone for decades.

"Alright," Jenna said, "what's this big secret you think I'm going to need a whole day to process?"

I was too tired to ease her into it, so I just stated it flat out, "Elise is pregnant. She says Jalen is the father. According to Jalen, it is actually a possibility."

Jenna's eyes widened, and her mouth opened, but no sound came out. I had to admit, her being speechless wasn't something I ever thought I'd see.

"Well, I definitely didn't see *that* coming." She gave me a close look. "Is this the sort of thing where the girl code requires I offer to cut off his balls? Because I don't have a problem with castration. In fact, I can turn them into a nice keychain for you if you want."

I gave her a thin smile. "Thank you for the offer, but he didn't cheat on me. They hooked up before he and I ever met. What I would like is to have breakfast with you tomorrow and talk about everything that happened in the past week and a half."

"Are we talking sounding board or serious life advice?"

I snorted a sound that was part bemused, part sad, and part sarcastic. "Right now, I'd be happy if my head didn't feel like it was going to explode."

"You can come by whenever you're ready," Jenna said. "No invitation necessary."

I thanked her, relief flooding my body. I'd known that if anyone could understand what I needed, it would be Jenna. I got out of the car and made my way to my steps, pleasantly surprised to find them brushed clean. A long hot soak in the tub, a mug of hot cocoa, and a good book were just what the doctor ordered. Everything else could wait until tomorrow.

"IT'S AMAZING how far a shower and a good night's sleep goes toward making a person feel human," I said as I followed Jenna from the doorway into the kitchen. "Are the kids with Suzette again?"

"With Zeke, actually," she said. "After they got home last night, Diana broke down in tears because they hadn't gotten anything for Suzette since she'd been with them. Rylan called Zeke, and now he's taking the kids for shopping day number two. He promised them ice skating and cocoa too, so they'll be gone a while."

She poured us each some coffee, then glanced at me. "Do you need something a bit stronger mixed in?"

I shook my head. "I'm appreciating not having anything fucking with my head."

A dark shadow crossed Jenna's face, and I knew I didn't have to explain what I meant. She understood. Then her eyes darted from one arm to the other, and I realized that anyone could've guessed at my meaning, thanks to the marks Serge had left. She couldn't see them now thanks to my sleeves, but she'd seen them in the hospital.

"I'm surprised Jalen walked out of there without killing those bastards." She set a mug down in front of me, then put the other in front of where she sat. "I can't imagine how hard it was for him."

"For *him*?" I tried not to sound as annoyed as I felt. I was supposed to be here to talk to my friend about what I'd been through, not listen to how difficult it had been for my boyfriend... or whatever Jalen was now.

Her expression was serious. "I don't doubt you went through hell, but you didn't see him. When he realized you were gone...I've never seen anyone look so completely terri-fied and pissed off at the same time. In my defense, when I said it had to have been hard for him, I was actually talking about how much restraint it must've taken for him to walk out without beating the shit out of every one of those men."

I supposed I could give him that. Still, it wasn't the only thing about the series of events that I needed to talk about.

"How could you let him go undercover? He told you, right? What he was planning?"

"He didn't have to," she said easily. "I was the one who found where the auction was and told him about it. When no one would help us, we talked about what needed to happen, and we made a plan."

"Shit, Jenna. What were the two of you thinking?"

She raised an eyebrow. "We were thinking that you were about to be sold to some pervert who was going to make you his sex slave, and we wanted you back."

I sighed. "There were so many ways that could have gone wrong, you know."

"But it didn't."

I ran my finger around the rim of my mug. "There were dozens of girls there. Guys too. Did Jalen tell you that?"

"He did." Her voice was flat. "And it killed us both to leave them behind, but it was the only choice to make." Her eyes met mine, and I was surprised by the affection that accompanied the steel. "I'd do it again."

"Give me one more day, and I'll be ready to help you find them," I said.

Jenna nodded, pushing back ebony hair from her face. "I knew you would." She took a long drink from her mug. "Now, how about you tell me what the hell is going on with Jalen and that psycho ex of his."

AFTER LISTENING to me talk for nearly ninety minutes, Jenna still seemed to be more stunned by the revelation about Jalen and Elise's pregnancy-resulting tryst than she was about anything else. I supposed after everything in her past, hearing about a couple bastards drugging and holding a woman captive so they could sell her to the highest bidder wasn't as shocking as it was to me.

"You've had a hell of a couple weeks," she said finally. "But please tell me you're going to work things out with Jalen."

"I want to," I admitted. "I love him, Jenna, but he's going to be a father."

"Maybe," she reminded me. "From what I know about Elise, there's no guarantee that the baby is his. Or if she's even pregnant."

"That's true," I said. "I don't know for sure, but I can't spend nine months waiting to find out, so I can know how to respond. I can't spend all that time building something only to have it ripped out from underneath me."

"You think Jalen is going to dump you if he finds out the baby's his?"

I glared at her knowing smirk. "When you put it that way... no, I don't."

"I don't either," she said. "Look, I've known Jalen for a couple years, and I've never seen him look at anyone the way he looks at you."

I flushed and looked down at my hands. "I don't know about that."

"I do," she said quietly. "Trust me, Rona. If he loses you, it'll destroy him."

Before I could come up with a response to that startling statement, the doorbell rang, and Jenna excused herself.

Losing me would *destroy* him? He risked his life going undercover to rescue me. He paid a lot of money – I hadn't decided if I wanted to know how much – to get me out. He told me that he loved me, and I had no reason to doubt him.

But a child changed things, even if neither of us wanted to believe it.

People could lose those they loved. It happened all the time. I'd lost both of my parents, even if my father was still technically alive. I'd lost Anton. Friends and family members died. Lovers and spouses died. Couples split up, sometimes even when they were still in love.

And life went on. People survived their losses.

If walking away from me was the only way Jalen could be the father his child needed him to be, then I would let him go, and he would survive it.

"Rona."

I looked up to see Jalen standing in the doorway.

He would make it if we split up.

I wasn't as sure about my own survival.

THIRTEEN

"How'd you know I was at Jenna's?" We'd been riding next to each other in silence for at least ten minutes before I finally asked the question. "Did she call you?"

He cut me a sharp glance. "No. Jenna would never do that."

"Then how?" I pressed.

A bit of color crept into his cheeks. "Rylan. But in his defense, I'm very persuasive, and he probably didn't even think that you might not want me to know."

"It's not that," I protested. "I mean, it wasn't that I cared that you knew, I just..." I shook my head. "Shit. A week and a half talking to myself and various hallucinations and I completely lose my ability to carry on a normal conversation."

Jalen laughed, and the awkward tension between us eased a bit. After a few more seconds of silence, he spoke again.

"I know you've been through a lot, and maybe I should have waited until you came to me, but I..." He glanced at me again. "I missed you, Rona. Yes, I was terrified when you were gone, but once you were safe, it hit me how much I missed seeing you, talking to you."

I couldn't help it. No matter how much my brain told me to keep my hands to myself until we talked things out, I reached over and put my hand on his arm. "I missed you too."

"Can I ask something?" He seemed to steel himself. "Why didn't you come to me to talk? I would've listened to you about everything. I could have held you while–"

His voice cracked, and his hands tightened on the wheel. A moment later, we pulled into his garage, and the moment the car was still, he turned toward me, a foreign, pleading expression on his face.

"All I've been thinking since I left the hospital is that you're going through all of this, and I'm not there to go through it with you." He took both of my hands in his. "I failed you. You were on that street because of me. You were *alone* because of me. I should have stayed with you. Better, I should have taken you back inside and told Elise to leave. You should have been my priority."

I shook my head and gently pulled my hands away. "Your child should be your priority. I would never ask you to choose me over him or her."

He opened his mouth to say something, then shut it again. He got out of the car and came around to my side to open my door. He held out a hand, and after a moment, I took it, letting him help me to my feet. His eyes met mine as he threaded his fingers between mine and tightened his grip, and I knew he was waiting for me to pull away again. This time, I didn't.

"I brought you here because I wanted to show you something."

He didn't expound as he took me into the house. As we walked through, I looked around, half expecting it to be different than I remembered. A week and a half had to have been enough time for Elise to leave her mark, especially since she'd lived here not too long ago. Other than a few additional dirty dishes, everything looked the same. Either Elise hadn't made any changes in this part of the house yet, or something else was up.

We went up the stairs, and a flash of heated arousal sparked low in my belly. Logically, I knew there were things to talk about before I could fall into bed with him, but my body craved the contact, no matter how much I told myself that I needed to be strong.

We walked past his bedroom door and went into the second door on that side of the corridor. What had once been a guest room was now empty and painted a pastel yellow. Even without furniture, this would obviously be a nursery. A door to the right stood open, revealing the master bathroom that was attached to Jalen's bedroom. Another door on the other side of the room was open as well, this one to a smaller bathroom.

"Once the paternity test is done," he finally broke his silence, "I'll know whether this needs to be a nursery connected to my room and to a guest room, or if I can find another use for it. Maybe something a bit more... adult."

I shivered at the heat in his voice but pushed my desire down, so I could focus on the important part of what he'd said. "Has she moved in yet?"

"No. It won't be like that." He pulled me through the

master bathroom and into his bedroom, leading me over to a chair. I sat down, and he let go of my hand, so he could sit on the edge of the bed. "I did some research, and there's a non-invasive paternity test that's ninety-nine percent accurate, and it can be done any time after the eighth week. As soon as I knew you were safe, I scheduled an appointment for Elise and me to go to the doctor and get it done. I haven't gotten ahold of her yet to tell her about it, but by this time next week, we should know if I'm the father or not."

A week. Just a single week more of not knowing. I supposed if Jalen could handle that, so could I.

"And if you are?"

"Then I'll go to doctor appointments with her. I'll make sure she's taking care of herself. I'll furnish and decorate the nursery."

"And the other room?"

"I'll make sure it has everything a mother would need, but if Elise wants anything more than that, she'll have to bring it herself."

"She'll be living here then."

Jalen moved into a crouch and took my hands. "She will have a guest room while the baby's young so that neither of us has to try to do the feedings and all that alone. And if I need to get a nanny because Elise wants to travel around modeling again, that'll be the nanny's room."

I loved that he wanted to be involved in his child's life instead of just sending a check every month, but my feelings were tempered by the fact that I still didn't know where I stood.

"What about me?" I asked softly. "What role do I play here?"

He reached up to brush back some hair from my face. "Whatever role you want. I need you to be part of my life, Rona. If the baby is mine, I'll take care of him or her, but I want to take care of you too. I don't want to lose you because of a lapse in judgment before we met."

I was silent for a minute, collecting my thoughts as Jalen leaned back on his heels. "You can't do anything like you did at the auction. Never again. You can't put yourself in that sort of danger. You must put your son or daughter first. That's the only way this can work. If you promise me to keep yourself safe."

"I promise," he said sincerely. He put his hand over his heart. "Never again. Just, please, Rona, don't shut me out."

I held out my hand, and he took it, pressing it against his forehead.

"I was terrified," he said, his voice barely above a whisper. "I didn't know where you were, what was being done–" The last word cracked, and he took a shuddering breath. When he spoke again, he sounded much calmer. "What I was thinking isn't what's important. What you need is what matters."

I ran my fingers through his hair and leaned forward to kiss the top of his head. "Thank you for finding me. Thank you for coming for me."

He raised his head, our faces inches apart. "I will always find you. No matter what it takes." One corner of his mouth quirked upward. "Even if I have to break my previous promise about not doing anything stupid."

I couldn't help but smile in response. It wasn't a surprise to hear him say it that way, and I knew he meant it. He wouldn't have been the man I loved if he wasn't willing to put his life on the line when he thought it was necessary.

"Do you think you could stay here tonight?" Jalen asked. "I couldn't sleep last night, knowing you were alone at your place. I have plenty of rooms for you to choose from, and I promise I won't touch you. I just need to know you're here and safe."

For a moment, I couldn't figure out why he thought I wouldn't want him to touch me. Then, it hit me. The doctors wouldn't have told him anything about my examination, and I hadn't told him anything about what I'd been through. All he knew was that I'd been kidnapped by the sort of men who auctioned off women.

"They didn't rape me," I said quietly. He flinched, but I kept going. He had to know. "They hit me and drugged me, but they didn't sexually assault me."

He muttered something under his breath, but I didn't need to hear it to see the relief in every line of his body.

"I needed yesterday to process and rest," I said. "I needed earlier today with Jenna to vent. Right now, I need something else."

His hands went to my knees, and I could feel the heat through my jeans. "Anything."

I put my hands on his and pulled them up my thighs. "Make me feel alive."

He kept his eyes on my face as he undid my pants. I raised my hips and let him take my jeans and panties down at the same time. He tossed them aside and spread my legs, baring my pussy as he finally dropped his eyes.

"Lay back and relax," he said. "Let me make you feel good."

My eyelids fluttered as he kissed his way from my knees to my inner thighs, then switched to the other side. The faint scruff on his cheeks burned against my sensitive skin, and then something hot, soft, and wet was moving over even more sensitive skin. I closed my eyes and gave myself over to Jalen's talented mouth and hands.

He kept his hands on my hips, holding me still as he worked his tongue between my folds and as deep inside me as possible. His nose brushed against my clit, and I jerked at the contact. From the moment he'd touched me, every nerve cell in my body had come alive, buzzing with anticipation. It wasn't going to take much to set me off, and as his tongue traced around my opening, pleasure coiled into a tight ball, spinning faster and faster. A flick of his tongue across my clit, and I came.

"Ah!" My back arched, and my hips rose as I pushed myself against his mouth.

What had started as a breathless response to the welcomed release of endorphins turned into a half-scream as he fixed his lips around my clit and sucked hard. One climax became two, ripping through my body with a near-painful force.

I pushed at his head, desperate for respite even as my body craved more. He chuckled, the vibrations sending another wave of pleasure through me. He turned his face into my leg, letting my throbbing pussy have a break as he sucked on other soft skin, teeth worrying until I knew he left a mark.

"J," I gasped and tugged on his hair. "Inside me. Please."

He straightened, lips shining from my arousal. "Not yet."

He reached for my sweater, and I raised my arms to let him pull it over my head, leaving me in only my bra. That was gone a moment later, and Jalen ran his hands over my sides and up to cup my breasts.

"You're fucking gorgeous, you know that?"

He leaned down and took one of my nipples into his mouth. A long pull had me gasping and writhing beneath him. When he switched breasts, I grabbed his arms, dug my nails in. "Fuck, J."

"I love watching the way your skin flushes when you're aroused." His teeth scraped sensitive skin. "Do you want gentle and tender, or do you want it rough?"

I blinked, confused by the apparent change of subject. "What?"

His tongue flicked out, teasing the tip for a few seconds before sinking his teeth into the soft flesh of my breast. I yelped, and he laughed, lifting his head.

"Do you want me to fuck you soft or hard? Gentle or rough?"

"Hard. Rough." I dug my nails into his scalp, letting him see the greed in my expression. "Time for soft and gentle later."

The raw passion on his face slipped for a moment. "Are you sure I won't hurt you?"

I tugged him toward me. "Hard. Rough," I repeated.

His mouth came down on mine, and he wrapped his hand around the back of my neck, holding me in place even as his free hand dropped between my legs. I whimpered as he shoved two fingers inside me, and he swallowed the sound. The digits twisted, rubbed against the sides of my channel, prepared me.

I tugged at his shirt, wanting to see and feel the skin that I'd been dreaming about. He broke the kiss and quickly tossed his shirt aside. I made a pleased sound as I raked my nails over his chest, teased his nipples. He put his mouth next to my ear.

"Fuck yourself on my hand, babe. Make yourself come on my fingers, and then I'll let you have my cock."

His words made me moan, and the sound only increased when I obeyed. I moved my hips, let my inhibitions fall away. Jalen didn't see my scar. He didn't judge how I responded to his touch, how good he made me feel. When he told me to do something, I knew he wanted me to let go and do it, not to overthink things.

He brushed his lips across mine, then kissed my jaw. He bit down on my earlobe, and I cursed, scratching his shoulders.

"Damn, you're a little wildcat," he murmured, with more amusement than pain in his voice.

"Sorry," I breathed, bouncing my hips faster as I chased the fire growing in my belly.

"More," he growled as he yanked on my hair, baring my throat. His thumb pressed against my clit and I scratched him again. "Mark me, babe. Make it so I'll feel you for days."

Damn if that didn't just make me hotter.

He bit my neck, and I had the fleeting thought that I was going to have teeth marks where everyone could see them. The thought didn't last long though because his knuckle rubbed against my g-spot, and I was gone.

When I came back to myself, I was on the bed, and a smug-looking Jalen was stretched out next to me. His pants were on but undone, exposing the hard steel of his erection. His hand moved slowly over his cock, and I watched his thumb swipe across the head, taking a bead of pre-cum and smoothing it across his skin.

"See something you like?" he teased in a low voice.

"I don't know," I teased right back. I loved when he was like this. "Are you going to put that thing to some real use or just play with it?"

He moved over me so fast that I barely had time to register the movement before his weight was on me. I wrapped my legs around his waist, and that was all the urging he needed. He slid home with one smooth thrust, and we both went still for a moment, savoring the feeling of completeness that came with finding a perfect fit.

Then we were both moving. He drove into me with deep, punishing strokes, and I rose to meet him, each thrust sending sparks shooting through me. His muscles flexed and bunched under my palms as I ran my hands over every inch I could reach. Neither one of us spoke, but we didn't need to, not with the connection between us so thick and real that I could almost see it.

When I came this time, he followed right behind me, both of us clinging to the other, wanting nothing more than to prolong the moment. Every inch of me ached and throbbed, but the new sensations drove away the lingering pains I had from what'd happened before, just like being with him made everything else fade away.

As Jalen rolled us onto our sides, I curled into his embrace and smiled. Now, I truly felt safe.

FOURTEEN

"I DON'T KNOW WHERE YOU THOUGHT YOU WERE GOING, but you should have known that you wouldn't get far." Serge paced in front of me, a dangerous smile on his face.

The temperature in the room dropped, and my teeth chattered hard enough to make my jaw hurt. Goosebumps exploded across my skin, and I shivered, unable to stop. I couldn't tell if it was more from the chill in the air or the anticipation of pain to come.

"That's my Rona. Always trying to run away."

My father lurked in the corner, flipping a knife back and forth between his fingers. Blood dripped from the blade and ran across the floor toward me. I tried to move away, but my limbs were frozen in place. I couldn't leave, couldn't fight. All I could do was wait.

"I tried being nice," Serge continued. "Those were high-quality drugs. Plenty of people would've paid top dollar for a taste of what I gave you for free."

"Nice doesn't work with her," my father said with a rusty laugh. "You gotta practically kill the bitch to get her to behave."

"Fuck you." I glared at him. If all I had was words and expressions, I intended to use them.

"Come on, little girl, you know that's not how I do things," my father said. "Serge, however, might want to get a little taste before he sells you off. I told him you weren't a virgin, so it's not like he has to worry about spoiling the merchandise."

Serge grabbed my hair and pulled my head back. I liked it when Jalen did it, but this wasn't even close to the same. His breath was hot against my cheek as he spoke.

"I'm going to enjoy this," he said. "When I'm done with you, you won't be able to move without remembering me. I'll ruin you."

The last statement echoed in my head as I jolted awake. It was a nightmare, not a memory, but that didn't mean my pulse wasn't racing. I rolled over, but I already knew that Jalen wasn't there. There was something about him that made me hyper-aware of his presence, whether he was there or not.

I put my hand on his pillow anyway. It was cool, telling me he'd left a while back. Since we were at his place, I knew he wasn't running away because of some weird freak-out. I assumed it was work, but I trusted him, wherever he was.

He hadn't left me a note, but the robe and fresh towels in the bathroom told me he'd been thinking of me, and that was enough to make me smile. By the time I emerged from the shower, I'd shaken off the nightmare and was ready to get back to my normal life.

For me, normal life meant heading back to my PI office

and waiting for people to come in and hire me to follow their cheating spouses. I called a car to pick me up, but I wasn't stupid. I stayed inside this time, and when the car finally pulled into the driveway, I made sure the description matched what was on my phone. Then I took a picture of the car and the license plate, sent them to Jenna, Jalen, and Clay.

If I disappeared again, I'd make sure they had a trail to follow.

My driver was nice, and we made small talk as he took me to the office. Someone had already cleaned the sidewalk both in front of Burkart Investigations and my own building. The steps were cleared too. As I walked up to them, I checked my voicemail and listened to a call from Jenna. It looked like once I changed into something more professional, I'd be heading out to the Archer house.

Jenna was working with the FBI to find Serge and the other trafficked people, and that case took priority over everything else. It wasn't *quite* my normal, but it was close enough.

"I READ OVER YOUR STATEMENT," Agent Matthews said. "Have you remembered anything else that might help us find these guys?"

I almost told him that if his partner had listened to Jenna and Jalen, the FBI wouldn't have needed to find the traffickers in the first place, but I liked Raymond Matthews, as much as I knew him anyway. It wasn't his fault that Clay had blown off Jenna and Jalen. Based on the annoyed expression on the agent's face every time he looked at Clay, I had a feeling Clay had already been hearing it from him anyway.

"Unfortunately, nothing new," I said. "But if I think of anything, I'll let you know. Maybe something Rona and I find will jar a memory loose."

"Are you sure you should be working this case?" he asked. "In the FBI, we usually discourage working on cases we have a personal stake in."

I raised an eyebrow. "You do realize that both Clay and Jenna are my friends, which means they have a personal stake in this too?"

I caught Jenna's smirk out of the corner of my eye, but Clay didn't look amused. In fact, he'd barely made an expression since I'd gotten there. And he wouldn't look at me either. Everywhere but at me.

"You can call either me or Clay if you find something," Agent Matthews said to Jenna. "Make sure you're being safe. That comes first. I don't want to get in trouble for my CIs being in danger."

He sounded gruff, but I knew he was only looking out for us. Jenna had told me how hard he'd taken it when he'd found out I was missing. Not as hard as he would've if it'd been her, but he'd still felt like it was his fault somehow. I didn't tell him that I'd been walking away by myself in the snow because my boyfriend had just found out that his wife was pregnant with his child. The story didn't get any less awkward with repetition.

"I'm going to stay for a little bit," Clay said. "Just in case they have any questions about what they're supposed to be doing."

The look Agent Matthews gave him said he didn't believe it any more than I did, but he nodded and left. Clay remained awkwardly leaning against the counter, his gaze landing everywhere but on me.

"I'll spend the day coming up with the avenues we want to track," Jenna said, drawing my attention back to her. "Once I know what I need you to track down, I'll send you an email with a list of everything I want you to do. Don't push yourself, and don't put yourself in any danger." Her expression was serious. "I'm not kidding, Rona. If I think you're doing something stupid, I won't let you help me anymore."

I sighed and rubbed my temples. "I didn't realize you wanted a third child, Jenna."

She laughed. "Don't do anything that I'd need to mother you about and I won't do it. Besides, I think of myself as more like a big sister than a mother."

I sighed. "I really need to start reminding people that I trained at Quantico."

"But you didn't graduate," Jenna pointed out.

"Thank you for the reminder," I said dryly. "Yes, I wasn't thinking clearly, and I wasn't as careful as I should have been, but it's not like I walked into a cartel meeting or something like that. We don't know that me being taken had anything to do with any case we've worked on. All we know for sure is that it had nothing to do with my father."

"True," she agreed.

"It doesn't mean you need to be reckless," Clay finally spoke up.

I shot him a glance over my shoulder and couldn't quite curb my sarcasm. "Oh, are you talking to me now?"

A phone rang, and I looked back at Jenna. The expression on her face told me it wasn't someone she was expecting. She quickly excused herself, leaving Clay and me alone for the first time since the hospital. Hell, the first time I'd even talked to him since then.

"I haven't...*not* been talking to you."

"You didn't bother to call me to see if I'd made it home safe."

Clay jerked his chin in the direction Jenna had gone. "I knew she'd take care of you. Her and Jalen."

"It seems like they're the only ones taking care of me."

He winced. "I deserve that."

"Yeah, you do." I kept my voice even. "What were you thinking, ignoring them like that? You had to know that they'd do something drastic."

"I was thinking that they'd leave me a message before doing something stupid. All they said was that they thought they might have found you and that they needed to show me something. They didn't tell me that Jalen was going to put himself into danger." He might've sounded like he was being defensive, but I could see the guilt on his face.

At one point in time, I might've thought he'd been punished enough, but he hadn't just put me in danger. He put the man I loved into danger because he'd been too arrogant to think that they might be able to do something better than he could. He said he wanted me safe, but he'd let his pride get in the way. I was angry at him, but more than that, I was hurt. Our sexual relationship had ended, and I'd thought we'd moved past it. We were friends – family really – but when it had come down to it, he'd ignored a lead because he'd thought he knew better.

"I want us to be a part of each other's lives," I said quietly. "I value your friendship and everything you've meant to me over the years, but it's going to take some time for me to not be pissed at you."

"I really thought I was doing the right thing," he said.

He finally looked at me, and I let our eyes meet.

"I know," I said with a sad smile. "And that's what I need to work through before things can ever be right between us."

FIFTEEN

I WOULD'VE PREFERRED TO STAY AT THE ARCHER HOUSE for a couple hours, get a list of things to do from Jenna, then go out and do them, but that wasn't really my call to make. Jenna had come back to the kitchen shortly after Clay left, but she hadn't asked where and why he'd gone. I knew some of her reasoning had to do with the fact that she'd just gotten off the phone with her sister, but I was also pretty sure that she knew I didn't want to talk about what was going on with Clay and me. I returned the favor and didn't press her about the phone call.

I'd gone back to the office then. Jenna had needed time to process her conversation with Stacey. Even if it'd been about something simple, the sheer strangeness of talking to a sibling she'd only ever imagined meeting had to have been jarring at the very least. Knowing her personality, she probably processed best by working, but she didn't need me hovering over her, impatiently waiting for her to find something for me to do. I told her that I'd be there if she needed to talk, and then I'd gone home.

I might not have had an FBI case to work on, but I did have a case. Yes, I wanted to save those people who'd been left behind at the auction, but there wasn't anything I could do yet. I had my own part to play, and I'd play it when I had the information I needed. Until then, I'd do the job I'd been hired to do and find Jenna's siblings.

A little over eight years ago, Jenna's mother had been pregnant with her last child. According to all the reports, that child had been stillborn. However, my conversation with Harry Franklin, a former US Marshal who'd been working on Helen Kingston's case, made me believe that might not have been the case.

Unlike Stacey and the other kids who'd been removed from Helen's custody, I wasn't going to be dealing with sealed adoption records and things like that. If Helen had indeed given birth to that last child while she was missing from Marshal custody, she wouldn't have handed it over to Child and Family Services in whatever state she'd ended up in back then. If she'd just wanted to give the baby up, she would've just stayed where she was. She'd left for a specific reason, and I was certain it had been to sell her child.

I just really hoped she hadn't sold the baby to the sort of people she'd been involved with before. Not only would that make it nearly impossible to find the child, but the thought of the life that kid would've led...it made me sick. It was sad that the best option to hope for was that she'd sold the baby on the black market to a couple who'd desperately wanted a child, but to whom traditional methods hadn't been an option.

Whoever she sold the baby to wouldn't have been able to

just magically have a child appear without certain information. Birth certificate, social security number, all that sort of thing. They would've needed to find that information somewhere, and it wouldn't have been legal.

Finding places where the parents could've bought those documents would've been a lot easier if I'd had Jenna's help, but I hadn't been hired to only do the easy things. I would do everything I could on my own and only involve her as a last resort.

It was time to get to work.

I HADN'T MADE a whole lot of positive progress by the time I was ready to call it a day, but I'd been able to eliminate some of the non-possibilities. If I didn't catch a lucky break, who knew how long it would take me to find a missing eight-year-old in a country of billions. Still, I was feeling pretty good about the way things had gone, especially considering it had felt like a normal day for the first time in a long time.

And then I saw Jalen waiting in front of my door and, for a moment, I thought things were going to end on a positive note. Then I saw the tight expression on his face, and I sighed.

"Come on in," I said as I unlocked the door. "You've got to be freezing your ass off out here."

"I haven't been waiting long," he said quietly as he followed me inside. "I didn't want to interrupt your first official day back at work. But it doesn't look like I interrupted anything since you weren't at your office."

"I was there earlier." I kicked the snow from my boots,

then tugged them off. "While I'm waiting for Jenna to delegate, I'm working on her case, and I needed to do some things outside of the office."

"Where?"

I tossed a look over my shoulder. "What?"

"Where did you have to go?"

I frowned at him, caught off-guard by how flat the question had come out. "A few different places. Are you okay?"

He stared at me. "No, Rona, I'm not okay. I came here to see you because I wanted to make sure that you weren't wearing yourself out." He ran his hand over his jaw, scrubbing his palm against his stubble. "But you weren't here, taking it easy. Of course not. You were out there. By yourself. Maggie said you didn't even tell her where you were going."

I'd been grateful when I found out that Maggie Carlyle, the woman I hired to be my receptionist, had come into the office even while I was gone. She'd been on time, had kept everything organized and neat. And there was no reason at all that I should be annoyed that she told Jalen she didn't know where I was.

Except I was, and that just made me more pissed at Jalen for making me feel that way.

"It's my job, Jalen," I snapped.

"A dangerous job. You never should've been out there alone."

I sighed and shook my head. "I trained with the FBI, then with Adare. I've been alone since my uncle died. I can take care of myself."

"Clearly, you can't."

I glared at him. "Dammit, Jalen! I wasn't working when those guys grabbed me."

"Don't remind me." The pain in his eyes was only matched by the guilt. "You made me promise to stay safe and not do anything stupid, but you apparently don't need to give me the same courtesy."

"That's different."

"How?" His voice rose.

"I'm not a parent. You have to think about your baby."

He cursed, his eyes flashing. "We don't know that it's my baby. And it doesn't matter. Serge is still out there."

My skin crawled just hearing the bastard's name, which turned my anger up another level. "I know that! I know he's out there, but I'm not going to let him keep me from doing my job." I took a step toward Jalen, needing him to see. Needing him to understand. "When things get tough, I run. I leave before people can leave me. Not this time. This is *my* life, J."

"And *you're* my life." He put his hands on either side of my face. "Don't you understand that? You're everything to me, and I can't lose you."

All my anger fell away when I saw the truth on his face. He wasn't trying to be petty, or even pulling some man versus woman thing. He wanted to take care of me because I was important to him. It was one thing to hear him say that he loved me, and it was something else entirely to see it play out.

"All right," I said, forcing my muscles to relax. "I'm sorry. I'll be more careful."

He crushed me to his chest and kissed the top of my head. "Please do. Otherwise, I might be forced to put myself in danger again, and we both know you'll be pissed if I do that."

I chuckled, and when he joined me, the knot in my chest

vanished with my anger. Things were going to be okay. We were going to be okay.

SIXTEEN

With Christmas coming up and so much work to do, I was a little surprised when Jalen said he wanted us to go out on Saturday evening, but I was also eager to do something fun. With all the seriousness behind the work I was doing, having a date like a regular couple sounded like exactly what I needed. We'd gone to dinner, but he hadn't told me what we'd be doing after. I'd assumed a movie or maybe a club to listen to some live music.

What I hadn't expected was for him to take us outside the city limits and up a winding driveway, past a sign that said *Hampton Acres Christmas Tree Farm*.

"A Christmas tree farm?" I shot him a surprised look.

He didn't say anything until he parked in front of a large, rustic-looking barn, the expression on his face telling me that he wasn't ignoring me, but rather figuring out how to tell me whatever was in his head.

"I didn't have a bad childhood," he said. "When my parents were together, we celebrated Christmas as a family.

When my dad left, it was just my mom and me, but it was good then too. The presents weren't overly expensive, but I never had anything to be ashamed of either."

I understood exactly what he meant. My family had been the same, even when I lived with Anton. Comfortable, but not excessive. We'd lived such different lives, but some things had still been the same.

"The one thing we never had, though, was a real Christmas tree. My mom's allergic to them, and even though I understood why we hadn't been able to get one, I still always wanted one." He gave me a sideways smile, the kind that let me see what sort of child he'd been. "I guess that's something all kids feel at one time or another. Sometimes we make up for lost time when we're adults, but Elise never wanted the mess, and I didn't see the point of putting one up just for myself."

My heart squeezed in my chest. "So, we're here to get you a Christmas tree?"

He leaned over and kissed my cheek. "We're here to get both of us Christmas trees." Suddenly, he frowned. "You're not allergic to pine, are you?"

I placed my palm on his beautiful face. "We used to get real trees when I was little. Before my father's...accident. The first Christmas it was just Anton and me, we tried a real tree, but it brought up too many painful memories. Every time I smelled it, all I could think about was the last Christmas we'd all been together."

"I'm sorry," he said. "I didn't know. We can go do something else."

"No, no, that's not what I meant." I hurried to reassure him. "It doesn't have the same effect on me as it used to. I

could go back and get it after I put this one in the house. I don't want you to feel like you have to stay tonight if you'd rather go home and decorate."

I put my fingers against his lips, stopping the flow of words. I understood what was driving him to keep talking, because it was in my mind too. Our date had begun as something sweet and simple, a way to celebrate the season together, but somehow, it had become so much deeper. With everything else that had been going on, it all somehow felt more important than it should have.

"The tree will keep for a bit," I said. "Let's go inside, get something to drink, then see what time it is before we decide what to do next."

He nodded, and I could see relief on his face. "Spiced wine?"

I shrugged. "Never had it before, but sure."

We left his tree strapped to the roof of his car and headed inside where I soon learned that I liked spices, and I liked wine, but I didn't like the combination of the two. Fortunately, Jalen wasn't offended when I asked for a glass of just wine. In fact, I thought he looked a little relieved as he poured us each a glass and then settled on the couch next to me.

I leaned against him, and he slid his arm around my shoulders. He'd turned on some music when we first came inside, and it made for nice background sound as we sipped our wine. As much as I'd enjoyed our date, this was nice too. I could relax here with him and not worry about all the things that wanted to crowd into my head.

"I like this," he said as he set aside his glass. "Being here with you at the end of the day."

"Me too," I said.

I turned my face into his chest and breathed in, filling my lungs with the scent of him. The faint smell of laundry detergent under the clean sweat from our long walk. Pine and snow. And him. All of it merged into something that made my belly clench and the space between my legs throb.

He brushed his fingers through my hair. "It's a couple inches longer than it was when we first met."

I shifted so that I could look up at him without losing the contact between us. "I used to have it short, but when I left Quantico, I grew it out."

He studied my face for a moment, and I wondered if he was trying to picture me with short hair. "I think you'd look good with any length hair, but I can't lie and say I don't like being able to use it."

His eyes locked with mine, and he wrapped his fingers in my hair, tighter and tighter until I let out a hiss of pain. I didn't understand how he knew exactly how far to take me, how much was enough. I didn't know where the line was, but he'd never crossed it, never made me ask him to back off. Something in his gaze told me he was about to dance close to it, and damn if the thought didn't make me wet.

"We don't have to do anything," he said, his voice low. "We can finish our wine, bring in my tree, decorate it, and then I can take you home. It will still have been a great night."

"It will," I agreed, "but I think we can do better than great."

Using my hair, he maneuvered me to the floor, positioning me on my knees between his legs. His gaze flicked to the bulge in his jeans, then up to my face, telling me all I needed to know about what the next step should be. My hands shook as I reached for his zipper, but it wasn't nerves or fear. It was pure anticipation.

I freed his cock, licking my lips as it came into view. Jalen groaned, his grip on my hair tightening. A zing of pleasure went through me, and I leaned down, darting my tongue out to taste the tip.

"Fuck!" Jalen growled, his hips jerking.

The pressure against the back of my head told me what he wanted, but I knew he'd wait for me to let him know it was okay. I nodded and waited for him to guide me again. I rested my hands on his knees, sliding them up his thighs as he pushed my head down. The muscles in his legs bunched beneath the denim, reminding me of just how strong this man was, and how good. Even now, taking control like this, he kept his strength in check, careful to never take things to the point where he was truly hurting me.

I opened my mouth only wide enough for the thick shaft to pass between my lips. He stopped me halfway, and I circled his cock with my tongue, tracing every inch I could reach. His breathing quickened, and he yanked on my hair again, making me take him deeper. I almost gagged as he reached the back of my throat, but I managed to relax by reminding myself that he'd stop if it was too much. Little by little, his cock disappeared into my mouth and throat until my nose brushed against the dark curls that surrounded the base.

"Fuck, Rona." The words came out choked, as if he was the one who could barely breathe.

He pulled me up, his dick falling from my mouth with a wet sound. It bobbed in the air, slick and full, and I wanted nothing more than to climb on his lap and sink down on it.

Then again, there was something I wanted more. I wanted to please him, which meant I'd wait until he told me what he wanted of me.

"You've got such a hot mouth," he said, running his thumb across my bottom lip. "I want to come in it. Watch you swallow every drop. I want you to taste me on your tongue when I take you upstairs, lick you until you're begging for release, and then take your ass."

Shit. Hearing him talk like that was almost enough to make me come. "Yes, please," I said, my voice ragged from desire or from taking him into my throat. More likely both.

He put both hands on my head this time, guiding me down until the tip brushed my lips. I opened again, but he didn't push me further. Instead, he raised his hips, driving his cock into my mouth fast enough to make me cough. He hesitated, and I gave him a thumbs up, the only way I could think to let him know that I was okay. He gave me a wicked sort of smile before his hips snapped forward. He kept his eyes on me as he held my head in place, fucking my mouth. Some of the thrusts were deep, and I struggled to keep from pushing him away, but others were shallow, and I used my tongue to give him extra friction.

"I'm going to come," he warned, the words low and rough. "Swallow it all, and I'll make you come twice before I take your ass."

I wrapped my lips tight around him and sucked hard. He cursed, and I let my teeth graze the sensitive skin, giving him what he needed to explode. His cum flooded my mouth, and I swallowed the salty liquid, remembering his promise. I looked up at him and knew that even if he hadn't made it, I would have done the same just to see that look of bliss on his face.

Jalen was, though, a man of his word.

After a few quiet minutes where he waited for his legs to start working again, he pulled me to my feet and kissed me, a deep and thorough kiss that left no room for doubt about how much he'd enjoyed what I'd done. When we were both breathless, we went upstairs to his room, and he set to work making good on his promise to give me two orgasms.

As I came down from my second toe-curling climax of the night, I became aware that Jalen had left the bed and was rummaging around in a drawer. It was only then that I remembered the second part of what he'd said, what would come after my orgasms.

"Bend your knees and hold your legs open," he instructed as he came back over to the bed.

I did as he said, flushing at how the position exposed me. It wasn't embarrassment, really, but rather a feeling that I *should* be embarrassed, that I shouldn't *want* him to do this. I wasn't a prude, and I didn't have any moral objections to anal sex. It was the trust that went with it. The trust that he would make me feel good. That this wasn't a form of humiliation but rather of intimacy.

"If you want me to stop, just say the word and I will," he promised as he knelt on the bed. "This will be a bit cold."

"Oh!" I yelped as he slicked something cool and wet against my anus.

"It'll warm up in a minute."

My eyelids fluttered as he pressed the tip of his finger against the ring of muscle and pushed. The familiar burn made me squirm, but Jalen didn't stop. He moved his finger in and out, twisting it until I became used to the sensation. I moaned as he added a second finger, turning burn into pain. A bearable pain that I knew would eventually bring me pleasure. He repeated the same twisting strokes, spreading his fingers on every other thrust.

"You can let go now," he said when he finally removed his fingers.

My legs dropped to either side, muscles quivering. He was hard again, and as I watched, he coated his cock with the same liquid he'd used on my ass. He leaned over me and took a nipple between his lips. He sucked on it with long, steady pulls that sent bright bursts of light across my nerves.

I ran my hands up his arms, tracing each muscle as I went. I felt the strength in them, the power, and marveled at the man above me. My palms skimmed across his broad shoulders and up his neck until I buried my fingers in his hair, held his head to my breast. A hand moved between my legs, thumb stroking my clit until I'd almost forgotten what he'd been preparing me for.

Then he raised his head, his heated gaze on my face, and I remembered. The blunt head of his cock pressed against my ass, and I tensed.

"Relax," he said softly. "Just look at me and relax."

As contradictory as it seemed, I forced myself to simply let go, then groaned as my body yielded to him as his cock pushed inside. I curled my fingers, my nails biting into his shoulder even as he went deeper. The sounds the fell from my lips were little more than noise, mewls, and gasps that joined the curses Jalen gave with each inch he moved forward.

He sank the last bit and held there, his body shaking

against mine. I wrapped my arms and legs around him, clinging to his body even as mine struggled to decide what it wanted. I'd never been so full, so overwhelmed with all the sensations my brain was trying to process. I wasn't sure how much more I could take, but I didn't ask him to stop. I wanted everything he could give me, even if I couldn't bear it.

I cried out as he rocked against me, even that slight movement sending another burst of pain and pleasure through me.

He stilled immediately. "Did I hurt you?"

I shook my head. "No. Please, J. Keep going."

I rolled my hips, gasping as I moved. And then he was moving too, our bodies gradually coming together at first, then with more purpose as we adjusted to the new way we fit together. His mouth came down on mine, teeth harsh and bruising against my lips. I would be sore tomorrow, but all I wanted him to do was hold me tighter, fuck me harder, be rougher. I wanted him to mark me indelibly, make me his.

Because I was his.

I'd told him before that I loved him, and that had been as true then as it was now, but this was beyond love. It was the need to belong. Not to a place or to a family, but to him. To belong to him and him to me.

The thoughts came with startling clarity, exploding into my mind even as I came. I didn't know what it meant, but I'd think about it later. Right now, I was too full of everything else that was him, and something had to give. So I gave myself.

Completely and totally, holding nothing back.

SEVENTEEN

I WAS MISSING SOMETHING, AND IT WAS DRIVING me nuts.

I'd hoped that taking the weekend off to spend time with Jalen would be the break I needed to see the investigation from a new angle this week, to see what I was missing. Except now, I stared at my whiteboard and tried to see whatever connection was slipping through my fingers.

Helen Kingston had managed to escape from Marshal custody twice. Granted, she hadn't exactly been living in the same house with her assigned Marshal, but people in WITSEC had rules to follow, meetings to keep, especially ones like Helen who'd been put under protection not because she was a witness but because of her own criminal history and connections. I talked with Marshal Franklin about what happened, and at the time, I thought that I'd gotten everything. Now, I wasn't so sure.

And I couldn't figure out how she'd done it. She wasn't stupid. The fact that she'd run a child pornography ring for more than a decade without getting caught was proof of that. But was she smart enough to have been able to leave Cheyenne without a trace, then return, claiming that she'd simply been going on a trip? And why had she done it? Had she simply been wanting to prove that she could? Had she miscarried like she claimed, or had she decided to have the child but hadn't wanted anyone else to tell her what to do with it?

All of those were good questions, but I couldn't help feeling like there was a question I should have thought of.

Harry had watched over Helen for more than thirteen years without incident, but then, eight years ago, Helen managed to slip away, have a child, then return, all without him knowing. He'd been a scapegoat, but he also felt guilty because he'd let her manipulate him into more lax monitoring and then he hadn't reported her absence. He'd looked for her himself for two weeks.

Only now, I was wondering if Marshal Franklin had left something out. Or, rather, someone.

That was it. The thing I was missing wasn't a thing but a person.

In thirteen years, Harry had to have taken time off. A sick day here or there wouldn't have been a problem, but he'd surely taken at least one vacation of more than a couple days. Which meant he would've had another Marshal looking after her while he was gone.

What if that other Marshal had been the one in charge of Helen when she disappeared that first time? If Harry had suspected that she was going to run or that she'd harm her child, and he hadn't told the other agent, he might have been willing to protect him or her out of guilt.

Or maybe the other agent had done more than miss something.

Shit.

I ran my eyes over the board again, seeing the facts line up with that new theory in mind.

An agent who looked the other way while Helen found a couple to buy her baby. Or maybe just a single person. An agent who might have been able to tell Helen where she could find someone to get her the paperwork to go along with that baby, or how to get away unseen. An agent who, maybe, had even helped.

I didn't like the idea that someone in the Marshal service had helped someone like Helen, but it made sense. The pieces fit together better with an unknown agent in the mix, and that told me that I wasn't completely crazy to be thinking along those lines. It also made Harry's decision to not fight being the scapegoat more understandable.

How to find my mysterious agent, however, was going to be a little more...difficult.

Harry Franklin hadn't been thrilled to see me before. Whoever he was protecting was important to him. I doubted he'd answer any questions I might give him this time, which meant I needed to go around him. At this moment, I could only see three possible options to do that.

One, ask Jenna to hack the US Marshals servers.

Two, petition the Marshals as a private citizen.

Three, ask another government agent to request the information.

I sighed and looked at the clock on the computer. If I left right now, I could make it to Clay's office by lunch. Tomorrow was Christmas Eve, but I knew Clay would be working. He always volunteered to work the days around Christmas so that agents with kids could take vacation time. That's what he claimed anyway. I'd always suspected that he also did it to give himself an excuse to avoid spending much of the holiday with his parents. He loved them, but I'd always gotten the impression that things were strained between them for some reason.

I didn't want to drive from Fort Collins to Denver in the snow and on the day before Christmas Eve, but of the three options, this one was the best. I could've called, but a favor like this warranted an in-person visit.

"I'll be out of the office for a while, maybe even the rest of the day," I announced as I stepped out into the reception area. "I need to head to Denver for a lunch meeting, and depending on where things go from there, I might be back or not."

Maggie nodded, blonde curls bobbing with the movement. "Do you want case calls forwarded to your cell or have me take a message?"

"Take a message for anything new, but if Jenna calls, have her call my cell," I said after a moment's thought.

"Do you want me to schedule appointments for any walk-ins or should I tell them I need to talk to you and I'll call them?"

"I don't want anything new scheduled this week," I decided. "Any walk-ins and phone calls, go ahead and schedule appointments for next week. Nothing on New Year's Day and nothing for the afternoon on New Year's Eve."

IT WAS STRANGE, realizing that I wanted to have the holidays off because I had someone to spend them with.

"Are we going to be closed then?" she asked.

I inwardly groaned. "I'm sorry, Maggie, I completely forgot to tell you. We'll be closed all day tomorrow and Christmas Day, as well as all New Year's Eve and New Year's Day." I felt awful. I couldn't believe I'd forgotten to let my lone employee know that she didn't need to come in on the holidays.

"I think you've been justifiably preoccupied," she said with a smile. "I'll hold down the fort here. Drive safe."

I smiled and thanked her before heading out into the wintery morning. She'd found someone to clear the sidewalk and parking lot, and we hadn't gotten a fresh layer since yesterday afternoon, so the roads were clear as well. It was cold, but probably not cold enough to keep the salt from working. I hoped all of that added together for a pleasant drive. I needed to have my head together when I met with Clay.

***

"YOU WANT ME TO DO WHAT?" Clay stared at me across the table as if he hadn't heard my clear and pointed request.

I'd known showing up at work with a lunch offer was a risk, but I'd also known that it'd be harder for him to refuse if we were face-to-face. Harder, however, didn't mean impossible.

"I need the names of all the US Marshals who had any contact with Marcy Wakefield."

"You mean Helen Kingston? Jenna's biological mother."

I nodded. "You gave me Harry Franklin's name, and I know he's the one who took the blame when Helen slipped under the radar and came after Jenna, but I don't think that's the whole story."

Clay drained his coffee and waved the waitress over for another, not speaking again until she walked away. "I'm going to need a little more than that if I'm making that sort of inquiry. The name of the main agent who fucked up, that wasn't too hard to get. I can make a call and get the information you want, but if I'm going to poke around that case, I need to know what's on the line."

Fair enough.

"A little over eight years ago, Helen disappeared for a couple weeks. She was pregnant when she left but wasn't when she came back. She claimed she'd been visiting friends when she'd gone into labor and delivered a stillborn. She had a death certificate, but said she'd had the baby cremated and scattered the ashes."

"You don't think she was pregnant?" He shook his head and changed his stance. "No, you don't think the baby was stillborn. Right?"

I nodded. "I think she left before she was due and stayed away until she had the baby, which I think she then sold."

A sick look settled on Clay's face, and I knew he was thinking the same thing I had at first.

"I don't think she sold the baby to anyone who'd have hurt it," I explained further. "I think she was too greedy for that. I'm willing to bet that a desperate couple who wants to adopt but can't for some reason or another would pay more than a trafficker."

"That makes sense," he agreed, "but why do you need to know who else had been in contact with her?"

"Harry never reported that she'd gone missing for a couple weeks. He told me it was because he was worried he'd get in trouble for lax monitoring. Then when she took off a second time to go after Jenna, he finally said something. It doesn't make any sense. Why would he be willing to risk this baby's life when he's the one who worked so hard to keep her from hurting the others she gave birth to while in WITSEC?"

"You think he's protecting someone," Clay said. "Another agent."

"Exactly. I think it wasn't Harry's fault that Helen left that first time, but he took the blame for someone else." I popped the last bite of my garlic knot into my mouth.

Clay studied me for a moment before speaking again. "You don't think it was an accident, do you?"

"I don't," I admitted. "I think that Helen had help leaving. I think she had help finding a couple, getting a fake death certificate for herself, maybe even a fake birth certificate and adoption papers for the parents."

"Shit, Rona, you're just asking for trouble." Clay leaned back in his chair. "You're going to accuse the US Marshals of aiding a known criminal in illegal activities while in witness protection?"

When he said it like that, it sounded a lot worse than how I'd been thinking it. "It's not my job to police the Marshals," I said. "I was hired to find people, and that's all I intend to do. If someone really is guilty, I'll hope they confess, but I'm not trying to build a case or anything here."

He rubbed his chin, a gesture I'd come to recognize as

one of his tells. He didn't like what I was doing, and he certainly didn't like that I'd come to him about it.

"Is there any way you can narrow it down to a smaller timeframe?" he asked finally. "I think making it too broad is going to raise red flags, and I can't have it looking like the FBI is interfering in Marshal business."

"Try nine and ten years ago," I said. "And thank you, Clay."

He sighed and pushed back from the table. "I did some profiling for the Marshals a couple years ago, helped them with a pretty tough case. I can call in a favor or two. Give me twenty minutes, and I'll know if it's feasible."

I thanked him again and ordered a piece of warm apple pie and ice cream to have while I waited. I barely had time to finish it before he was back, his coat dusted with snow and his cheeks red. He shivered as he sat down and called over the waitress. She refilled his coffee, then took his dessert order. After she left, he took a long drink, then turned his attention to me.

"Nine years ago, Harry Franklin was partnered with a twenty-five-year-old newbie named Salome Balk. She wasn't just any new Marshal though. Balk was the daughter of Franklin's former mentor and partner who'd been killed in the line of duty ten years before that."

Shit. He *had* been covering for someone. I hadn't realized how little I'd believed my own hunch until I registered surprise that I'd been right.

"It gets better," Clay continued. "Part of what Salome was supposed to do was handle things if Harry was away or sick. He'd officially put in for vacation time for two weeks around when Helen disappeared, and he didn't show back up on the clock until his vacation was over, but the guy I just talked to said that Harry had been seen in Cheyenne halfway through the week even though he'd told everyone he was taking his wife to Niagara Falls."

"He came back because Salome lost Helen."

"That's what I think," Clay said. "The final nail in the coffin is what happened to Salome when Helen came back. Without any sort of explanation or warning, she quit her job and went back to school to be a nurse. She said she'd realized that healing people was her calling, not being a Marshal, but I think she couldn't handle the guilt of betraying Harry and of being responsible for the loss of Helen's baby."

"I can work with guilt." I said it mostly to myself, but it was loud enough that Clay heard.

"Are you sure you want to do that?"

"If we're right about what happened, that means Salome aided a criminal in the black-market sale of a baby, then let her mentor hide what she'd done. She might have even helped Helen the second time Helen took off. I don't have a lot of sympathy for her."

I sounded harsh even to my own ears, but I meant it. I wasn't here on a mission to get Salome in trouble. That wasn't my business. My business was finding out what happened to that baby.

"I got her contact information," he said. He pulled out a piece of paper and jotted something down. "My guy said that he heard she moved to South Carolina a couple years ago to work as a rep for some big pharmaceutical company, but her cell number should be the same."

I took the paper and stuck it in my purse. "Thank you. I really appreciate your help."

"I'll always be here to help you," he said. He leaned forward, his expression earnest. "And I'm sorry I wasn't there for you before. I should have listened to Jalen and Jenna instead of thinking I had to find you on my own."

I held up a hand. "I don't want to talk about that. I appreciate everything you did for me, but I want to focus on my case."

He watched me for a moment, then nodded. "All right. I'll drop it for now, but I don't want what happened–"

"Please, Clay. I really don't want to do this now." I rubbed my forehead. "In fact, I need to go. I want to call Salome from my office."

I kept making excuses as I waved the waitress over. Clay tried to interrupt, but I talked over him. Things had been okay when I'd kept it to business, but I wasn't ready for anything personal. Not yet.

I was halfway home before my mind stopped racing back to Clay and the discussion that I knew was in our future. Finally, I was able to solidify my schedule for the rest of the day. I'd be back in Fort Collins before dinner, plenty of time to make my call before Jalen stopped by.

I'd been so caught up with finding a possible baby that I'd almost forgotten about the *other* baby. Jalen told me yesterday that he and Elise were going to the OB/GYN for their first ultrasound and the non-invasive paternity test he'd finally managed to convince her to take. With the holidays, the results would take a little longer to come in, but hopefully, by the first of the year, Jalen would know if the baby was really his or not.

I was in the middle of planning what I'd do for dinner when my phone rang.

"Hi."

"Hey, where are you?" Jalen's voice was tense.

"I'm on the way back from Denver. I needed Clay to get me some information for Jenna's case. Is everything okay?"

"Not really," he said with a sigh. "But I can wait until you get back. I don't want to distract you."

"I'm fine," I said. "The roads are clear, and the traffic's not bad. It's actually a pretty nice day for a drive."

The fact that he didn't argue with me told me just how serious it was. "Elise canceled the appointment."

I bit back the smart remark I wanted to make, telling him that I wasn't surprised that Elise had managed to avoid the paternity test. I even had my doubts about the pregnancy itself. I didn't say any of that though.

"What happened?"

"Apparently, she had the chance for a shoot, and since she wants to keep working as long as possible, she felt like she needed to take the job." I heard the frustration in Jalen's voice. "We had to reschedule for after New Year's."

Of course they did.

But I wasn't going to say anything. It wasn't my place. I would support Jalen's choices, but I wasn't going to add in my two cents. Not unless he asked. I'd listen and be there for him. No matter what.

THE WOMAN on the other end of the video call had dark, wavy hair, baby blue eyes, and a sweet face. Cute, but not overly memorable. She also had one of those faces that showed every emotion, and right now, she was nervous.

"I don't understand why a private investigator would want to talk to me. I work at a pharmaceutical company that donates money and resources to third world countries and low-income neighborhoods. They're good people."

"I'm sure they are," I said, "but I'm not calling about your current job. I'm calling about a job you had almost ten years ago. With the US Marshals."

The color drained from her face as I watched. "The Marshals?"

"Yes, Ms. Balk." I kept my voice even, devoid of judgment. No matter what I found out, I couldn't judge her, not if I wanted her to talk. "Specifically, I'm looking at the time you spent with Harry Franklin in Cheyenne, Wyoming."

Her eyes darted away from the screen, and she fidgeted, twisting her fingers together. "Um, I don't really know why you'd need to talk to me about any of that. I wasn't with the Marshals for long. A couple years and then I left."

"Why did you leave?"

"It wasn't for me," she answered quickly. Too quickly. "That's all. I thought it'd be a good fit because of my dad. He worked for the service for decades. Gave his life to it, and I thought becoming a Marshal would honor that memory, but I wasn't really much good at it."

She was rambling, but I let her go. Sometimes when people were talking out of nerves, they said things they wouldn't normally say.

"I'm not really a people person," she continued. "They act like they like me, but then they do things..." Her cheeks flushed.

Shit.

A suspicion formed, and my gut said to follow it. "Ms.

Balk, did you become...*involved* with someone you were assigned to?"

"No. No. Of course not. I never..." Her voice kept rising until it was shrill. "I wouldn't..."

"Ms. Balk, I was hired by one of the daughters of Marcy Wakefield, also known as Helen Kingston, to find Kingston's other children."

"I can't help with that," she said, shaking her head. "I don't know anything about that."

"I think you do." I kept my voice even. "I think Wakefield manipulated you, either by pretending to be your friend or something more. I think she fed you a story when she got pregnant eight and a half years ago, some story that made you help her."

I could see it on her face, the embarrassment and humiliation. I might have gotten some of the details wrong, but I was on the right track. Salome Balk was my missing piece, and she'd get me the lead I needed to find another one of Jenna's siblings. I couldn't do anything about Serge and the others right now, but I could do this.

EIGHTEEN

As soon as I got off the phone with Salome, I called Jenna. After everything she'd done for me, I wanted to tell her that I had a good lead on finding another of her siblings. I made a few moments of small talk before jumping into the real reason I'd called.

"It turns out that Helen figured since she couldn't seduce Harry Franklin into doing what she wanted, she'd try seducing the young woman who was Franklin's junior partner. She told Salome that someone in the Marshal service had forced himself on her and that was how she'd gotten pregnant. There was this whole sob story that Helen made up, and it was enough to convince Salome to help Helen 'save her baby.'"

I relayed the rest of our conversation, explaining how Salome had arranged for Helen to meet with a gay couple who had been excluded from adopting due to some issues in their past. She'd taken care of all the paperwork and had made sure Helen returned to Cheyenne. Once Helen had gotten back, Salome found out that she'd accepted money from the couple, but Salome hadn't been able to report it without revealing what she'd done. Franklin, however, had been suspicious.

"Fortunately for us, Salome remembered a lot of details about the couple, and it shouldn't take me long to find them. I might even have them for you tomorrow."

When I finally stopped talking, there was a long silence, and then Jenna said, "That's...a lot."

"I just thought you'd want to know that I should have another name for you soon."

"It's Christmas Eve tomorrow," Jenna said. "Wait until after Christmas to do anything else. Enjoy your holiday."

"I'm not really doing much of anything," I said.

"Yes, you are."

She sounded so sure of herself that it caught me off guard.

"Besides, you can't go around calling people on Christmas asking them if they illegally adopted a baby eight years ago."

"Well, when you say it like that," I said with a laugh. "You're right. I hadn't thought about it."

"Now that you know you can't work, you're free to do what you want for Christmas." Jenna paused, and then added, "And one of those options is for you and Jalen to come to Christmas Eve at our house. Rylan and I are having family over, and we'd love for you to join us."

"I can't intrude," I protested.

"You're not. You and Jalen are coming to our Christmas Eve party at six o'clock. We're going to have food and games, and unless you can tell me that you and Jalen are doing something else, you have no excuses."

She was right. About me at least. I hadn't talked to Jalen about what he was doing over Christmas. I couldn't even lie and say that I'd forgotten. I'd been too scared that he'd tell me that spending Christmas together would be moving too fast.

"Bring some wine. Jalen has a good selection."

And I apparently had another call to make.

NINETEEN

I'D NEVER GONE TO A CHRISTMAS PARTY BEFORE. ANTON had been invited to parties when I lived with him, but he'd always made a point of staying with me, trying to give me as normal a holiday as possible. After he was gone, I hadn't really felt like celebrating much.

I grimaced at myself in the mirror and tugged on my dress as if it needed help to lay correctly. I'd bought this dress on clearance a couple months ago and then forgot about it since it was clearly a winter dress. A deep, rich blue, it made my eyes stand out, and the material clung to my body. The neckline was high enough that my scar didn't show, but the plunging back and the high slit revealed plenty of skin. I hoped Jalen would like it as much as I did.

The knock on the door made me turn away from the mirror, and I took a deep breath. We'd said *I love you* but, somehow, this felt a little more serious. Like we were making a public declaration, showing up at a family thing together. Like we were saying *we* were family.

I pushed the thought away as I opened the door...and promptly lost the ability to think.

Damn.

His slacks were a deep charcoal gray and perfectly fitted to his long legs and narrow waist. The shirt was a cranberry red, just tight enough to show off his broad shoulders and muscles.

"Wow." Jalen broke the silence first. "You look...wow. I mean, you always look good, but that dress is amazing."

I blushed and ran my hands over my hips. "Thank you. You look great too."

"Shall we?"

He helped me into my coat and then held out his arm. I took it, and we made our way down the outside steps. We didn't talk much on the drive, but it was a comfortable silence, filled with soft Christmas carols and the low purr of the engine. Tension I hadn't even realized I was holding bled away with each mile so that by the time we reached the house, I was ready.

The Archers had decorated their house and property with strands of white and blue lights, lining their driveway to provide a clear path all the way up. When we were welcomed inside, the explosion of color made me smile. Red and green and gold were everywhere. Ribbons and tinsel and bows. Where the things outside had been clearly laid out, everything in here looked haphazard. Some of them were crooked, and the spacing was uneven. Through the living room archway, I could see the tree shining with bulbs and lights and tinsel, ornaments put on at random.

It was wonderful.

Even if I hadn't figured out the reason for the difference,

one look at the beaming little girl standing next to the tree would've told me. Diana was dressed in a red velvet dress with white lace, the sort of thing that I would've hated when I was her age, but it was clear she loved it.

Jeremiah didn't look quite as thrilled in his dress pants and shirt, but he had that half-embarrassed expression on his face that boys his age had when they were enjoying themselves but didn't want to admit it. He lingered near Zeke, hero worship shining in his eyes, and he gave us polite smiles when we greeted him, a far cry from the sullen boy I first met.

"Thanks for coming," Jenna said as she came forward to take our coats. She handed them off to Jeremiah and then took the wine Jalen offered. "Make yourselves at home."

"I love the decorations," I said to Rylan as Jalen and I followed him into the living room.

"Jeremiah and I did the decorating," Diana announced proudly. "Dad helped us with the top, but we told him where to put things."

"Yes, they did," Rylan said with a smile, his eyes dancing. "They were very bossy."

Diana put her hands on her hips. "You said we were allowed to be bossy with you as long as we didn't fight."

He bent down and kissed the top of her head. "Yes, I did, and you two were exceptional. No bickering at all."

She beamed, basking in his praise, and my heart clenched. I'd almost forgotten what it had been like to earn a father's praise. I had the memories of those good years, but a lot of times they hurt more than the bad ones, reminding me of what I'd lost rather than what I'd had. Seeing Diana with Rylan and knowing what that little girl had gone through in her short life reminded me of how good I'd had it. Being thankful for those years didn't excuse what happened later, and it didn't dishonor my mother's memory.

"Rona are you okay?" Jalen's hand on my back grounded me. "You looked like you were drifting for a minute there."

I smiled at him. "I was, but I'm back."

"Good," he said, "because I've just been informed that we're required to follow tradition."

I gave him a puzzled look and then followed his gaze as he looked up. Mistletoe.

"You have to kiss," Diana said. "It's the law."

A smile played around Jalen's lips, but when he spoke, his voice was serious. "We wouldn't want to break the law, now would we?"

I shook my head. "Definitely not."

He put his hands on my hips, his touch light but hot. My hands went to his shoulders as I tilted my head back. The kiss he brushed across my lips was chaste, but it sent a bolt of heat and desire through me nonetheless. The warmth settled low in my belly, simmering there with the promise of more intimate things to come, and it stayed as we ate dinner and saw the kids off to bed.

After my second glass of wine, I excused myself to use the bathroom. I'd spent time in the house before, but I hadn't really paid much attention to the pictures lining the hallway to the guest bathroom until now. Diana and Jeremiah's faces were everywhere. Some of the pictures were of all four of the Archers, and there were a few of Rylan and Jenna alone, including one of their wedding, but the majority were of the kids. A couple of them looked like they were school pictures, but most of them were candid shots. Diana exclaiming over a giraffe at a zoo. Jeremiah sitting in a classic muscle car at what appeared to be a museum. Both children building a snowman.

I stopped in front of a whole collage of the family working on a pair of bedrooms. They were painting the walls, and every picture showed them smiling and laughing together. The sight brought back a memory with enough force to make me tear up.

"Are you sure that's the color you want?" Dad sounded doubtful, but he'd promised me my choice, and I knew he'd keep his word. Even if he didn't like the mint green paint I'd chosen.

"Yes," I said firmly. "I want this on the walls and that one for the trim."

I was going to be ten next week, and as a birthday present, my parents had finally agreed to let me redo my room how I wanted it. No more pastel yellow walls or babyish curtains. I was even going to get a new bed, but Dad said that had to wait until after we painted because he didn't want to risk ruining it. I hadn't told him or Mom, but I was looking forward to painting almost as much as when the room would be done because all three of us were going to paint it together. Mom and Dad had been working so much lately that we never had time together. Sure, sometimes they could be lame, but unlike a lot of my friends, I still liked spending time with them.

I blinked, bringing myself back to the present. I'd almost completely forgotten about us doing my room together. We'd spent an entire weekend getting it done. We'd ordered pizza and ate on the floor like it'd been a picnic. I'd forgotten to pull my hair back at one point, and it'd stuck to the wall, getting paint all over it. Instead of being mad, my mom just laughed and dabbed paint on the beard my dad had been growing that year.

"I was beginning to think you'd gotten lost." Jalen came over and stood next to me. "Photogenic family."

I nodded. "Most of my family pictures are in storage in Indiana. Pretty much anything personal is there actually. Anton sold the house and most of the furniture, but he didn't have room in his loft for the rest, not knowing what I wanted to keep. He didn't want to be the one to decide what got thrown away, so he rented a storage unit. After he died, I put most of my stuff from the years with him in there too."

"My family really didn't do much in the way of family photos," he said, "as I'm sure you noticed."

I had, but it hadn't seemed like the sort of thing I should mention. I reached over and took his hand. "I've never been a big fan of having my picture taken."

He pulled me to him and wrapped his arms around me. "Does that mean I won't be able to convince you to pose for me sometime?"

The mischievous glint in his eyes told me he was teasing, but I appreciated the change from a topic that could've turned the mood maudlin.

"I don't know," I teased back. "I suppose I could be persuaded. If you worked really hard at it."

He glanced around us, then pulled me through a doorway and into the library. My head spun as he backed me against the wall, but he didn't give me a chance to steady myself before his mouth came down on mine. He made a pleased, hungry sound in the back of his throat as his tongue pushed apart my lips. I curled my fingers into his shoulders, clinging to him as he ran a hand down my side and over my hip.

"I'm going to make you come," he murmured as he slid his hand under the slit in my dress. "You're going to come on my fingers, and then we'll go back in to our friends and enjoy the rest of the party."

I nodded, a shiver running down my spine. His fingers danced, feather-light, along my skin even as he kissed his way across my jaw and down my neck. His teeth scraped against my skin, and I bit my lip to hold back the moan that wanted to escape.

He leaned against me, the flat planes of his chest hard against the points of my nipples. His fingers pressed against the front of my panties, and he chuckled. I didn't need him to tell me that the cloth was damp. He could make me wet with a single kiss.

I cried out as his fingers dipped under the elastic of my panties, two of them sliding inside me without any hesitation. He clamped his hand over my mouth, his eyes dark with desire.

"Shh," he said with a smile. "Can't be too loud."

I glared at him as he twisted his fingers, sending a jolt of pleasure through me. His thumb rubbed my clit with brisk, almost rough strokes, pushing me toward something explosive. Something jarring and brutal. I whimpered against his hand, squirming as he drove his fingers into me, my muscles quivering as the pressure built inside me.

"I want you to come," he practically growled the words. "Dammit, Rona, come. I need to see you come."

I cursed, the word muffled by his hand. My back arched, and I rocked against his hand. I squeezed my eyes closed, nails digging into the soft fabric of his sweater. He continued talking, ordering me to climax, telling me how much he needed to see it, how much he wanted to feel me come on his fingers. And then I was there, crying out his name as white-hot pleasure coursed through me.

TWENTY

"Do you have any idea how hard it was not to take you right there in the library?" Jalen said as he pushed his hands into my hair. His voice was gruff, his body hard as he pressed me against the door.

"I would've let you," I admitted, wrapping my arms around his neck.

"Fuck," he growled into my throat.

His hands dropped to my hips and slid around to cup my ass. The moment I felt him lift, I pushed up and wrapped my legs around his waist. He shoved my skirt up and rocked against me, his cock hard beneath his zipper, my panties wet as they rubbed my oversensitive skin.

"I need you inside me," I breathed against his ear. "Now, J. It's all I've been able to think about since you had your fingers in me. I want to come on that thick cock of yours."

He shuddered, back muscles rippling under my hands. "You keep talking like that, and I'm going to fuck you right here."

"Good." I bit his jaw, not hard enough to mark, but hard enough to sting.

He pulled back enough for our eyes to meet. "You better be sure you want this."

The warning made my pussy throb. "I want it."

He didn't look away as he reached between us. His zipper rasped down, and he pulled my panties aside. With one quick jerk of his hips, he buried his full length inside me, both of us cursing as we came together. He fucked me in short, fast thrusts, the base of his cock rubbing my clit with almost painful friction. I didn't ask him to stop though. I meant what I said. I wanted this. I wanted the edge that pain gave me, the extra intensity that came with riding that fine line.

I came quickly, my uninhibited cries echoing in the foyer. He followed a moment later, his cock pulsing as he emptied himself deep inside me. He kissed me then, softly, his hands gentle as they eased my legs down. I wobbled, my knees weak, and he chuckled as he caught me around the waist.

"Now that we've taken the edge off," he said, "what do you say we head upstairs and take things a little slower?"

"THAT'S NOT GOING TO FIT." I could hear the slight quaver in my voice, but it was understandable, in my opinion anyway. The butt plug in Jalen's hand was huge.

He raised an eyebrow and wrapped his free hand around his cock. "It's thinner than my dick, and that's been in your ass."

"Yeah, but not when I had something else in my pussy," I argued.

Even as I protested, a part of me was turned on by the idea he'd proposed, and if I was completely honest, it'd been something I'd always been secretly fascinated with. I'd never tried it. Like other things, it'd always required too much trust for me to do before, and then when I found a person I trusted enough, the idea of inviting someone else to join us wasn't something I wanted to consider. Jalen bringing it up had surprised me – and bothered me, truthfully – but only for the short length of time it had taken him to clarify. He didn't intend to share me. He'd use other means to accomplish the task.

Hence, the flesh-colored toy he was currently holding.

"Do you trust me?"

I sighed, but I wasn't annoyed. I'd simply needed him to give me an excuse to agree despite my nerves.

"I do."

"Then get up on your hands and knees. You don't want to end up on Santa's naughty list on Christmas Eve, do you?"

I shot him a dirty look as I got into position. "You're really going to invoke Santa's name for something like this?"

"Hell yes," he said, lightly slapping my ass. "What do you think I wanted for Christmas?"

I laughed, the sound turning into a yelp when a lube-coated finger breached my ass. He'd been playing with it a bit while he'd gone down on me earlier, but I'd had a feeling there really wasn't such a thing as genuine preparation for that initial anal penetration.

Then again, a lot of things about my relationship with Jalen hadn't stuck to my expectations.

My head dropped forward, hair falling in a curtain on either side of my face. Despite the cool liquid he trickled down my crack, the second finger he was currently working in burned. I let out a slow breath and tried to relax. He would make me feel good, I knew, but it was a process.

"You know," I said breathlessly, "I'm pretty sure *this* is what would get me on Santa's naughty list."

He laughed, that low, masculine sound that sent a rush of arousal through me. "I don't know about that. You look pretty nice to me, and I think even good old Saint Nick would agree with me if he saw you like this."

I flushed at the thought of what I must look like. Head down, ass up. Nipples jutting out from my breasts in two hard little points. Pussy dripping and clit swollen from him making me come with his mouth. His fingers moving in and out of my ass.

"Don't worry," he said, his free hand running the length of my spine. "No one but me will ever see you like this."

I told myself that he wasn't making any real promise, just talking in the heat of the moment, but I couldn't stop that bright flicker of hope that sparked at the thought of us being together always. A year ago, the idea of being in an exclusive, committed relationship would have scared the shit out of me, but now, with him, I could see it. Okay, it still terrified me, but it was a different kind of terrifying. The sort of anticipatory excitement that came with any unknown, but positive, adventure.

"All right," he said as he pulled out his fingers. "I want you to relax and let me do the work. If it's too much, tell me."

I closed my eyes as cool plastic pressed against my asshole. My legs shook as the pressure grew, but I didn't ask him to stop. I listened, instead, to the soft soothing sounds that he made and reminded myself that he wouldn't hurt me. Not really. The stretching burn that grew steadily as he pushed wasn't true pain.

I groaned as the hard shaft pushed past the muscle and slid into my ass. I couldn't hold back a whimper as it settled into place, my brain struggling to process the impulses my nerves were sending out.

He brushed the hair away from my face, his expression one of concern as much as it was of desire. "Are you okay?"

"Give me a moment."

He nodded. "Take all the time you need."

I wasn't planning on keeping either of us waiting that long, but considering the massive erection he was sporting, I appreciated his patience. His hand moved over my back, fingertips brushing the end of my scar. His touch soothed me, helped my muscles relax and adjust.

"Okay," I said. "I'm good."

"Are you sure?"

I raised my head and met his gaze. "Very."

He leaned down and kissed the corner of my mouth. "If it's too much–"

"I'll tell you," I finished the thought.

He smiled and moved behind me. A moment later, I gasped as a single digit slid into my pussy. As wet and turned on as I was, he should've been able to start with two fingers, but the plug changed things, making even one finger feel impossibly thick.

I lost all track of time as my world narrowed down to what he was doing to my body. Each stroke reached a new place, nudged me closer to pleasure, but before I got there, a second finger joined the first, and I went through the process again. He took me to the edge, fingers twisting as he brushed his thumb over my clit.

"I want you to come again," he said, pressing his lips to the base of my spine. "Come once more for me."

My breaths came in small pants, everything in my body focusing on that small knot of pleasure growing low in my belly. I could hear him talking, encouraging me, coaxing me, but his voice sounded like it was coming from far away, an echo in my head, and then it was all noise, a rush of blood in my ears, the pounding of my heart.

The muscles in my body clenched and the feeling of my ass spasming around the plug sent a shudder through me. I made an inarticulate sound.

"Good girl." He ran his hands over my hips and squeezed my ass. "Are you ready?"

If I could've managed to talk, I would've told him that was a silly question because I didn't think I could really be ready for what was coming, but all I could manage was a nod.

He ran the tip of his cock along my slit, teased it over my swollen clitoris. I shivered, then gasped as he eased inside. Just the head at first, his hips rocking back and forth as he gave me the time I needed to adjust. Inch by inch, he filled me, and he cursed each time I tightened around him. His arms slid around my waist, hands moving up to cup my breasts as he curled over my back.

"Fuck, Rona." His teeth scraped over my shoulder, and I shuddered, drawing another curse from him. "You feel so good, babe."

I moaned as his fingers teased my nipples, lightly tugging on them even as I squirmed under him. Too many sensations were trying to make themselves known. I couldn't sort them all out. Flames licked across my nerves, chasing prickles of electricity and pleasure. The pressure was almost overwhelming, the most intense thing I'd ever felt, but then he moved, and everything else flew away.

I couldn't explain it, but it went deeper than my skin, my nerves. It went clear to the bone, to my soul. It was beyond physical pleasure, something primal, a connection far beyond just sex. It didn't matter that I couldn't see his face or that we weren't making eye contact. We moved together in the sort of perfect unison that didn't happen often, at least not to me. A dance that we seemed to instinctively know the steps to.

When we came together, it was like nothing I'd ever experienced before, a feeling that carried through to when we collapsed together in a pile of tangled limbs. He wrapped his body around mine and pressed his lips under my ear. In a few moments, we'd need to move, to clean up, but for right now, I was content where I was.

TWENTY-ONE

RED AND GREEN LIGHTS LAZILY BLINKED, REFLECTING OFF the ornaments and the walls. Glass bulbs of varying colors and sizes hung from the branches, and the scent of pine filled the air. A few plaster ornaments hung there too, all messily painted by a child's hand.

My hand.

As soon as I was old enough to paint, my mom had put a brush in my hand and let me make my own ornament. It hadn't mattered that I'd painted the dog purple or hadn't separated its mouth from the ball it held. It'd been about the memories we were making. That's what they said. My parents. Decorating the tree was as much about memories as it was about how pretty it was when we were done.

This year, we hadn't painted anything. We made snowmen instead. Mom let me use a hot glue gun for the first time, and I burned my fingers, but it'd still been fun. Three cotton balls, one on top of the other. Two googly eyes and three *buttons. We made scarves and hats from some flannel material Mom had bought.*

They hung right in the front of the tree, all three of them. Mom, Dad, and me.

The presents were piled under the tree: Dad's gifts were wrapped in red, Mom's in green, and mine in purple. Mine were always in purple. It was hard to find purple holiday wrapping paper, but Mom always managed to do it.

They weren't up yet, but that was part of the tradition. I'd wake up and tiptoe downstairs, trying not to wake them up. Not until I made them breakfast. Every year, I got a little more ambitious. Last year, I made toast and cut up some grapefruit. This year, I was going to make cinnamon rolls. Mom had bought frozen ones for me to put in the oven. This was the first year I'd been allowed to use the oven by myself, but I still wasn't ready to make the rolls on my own.

Maybe next year.

It was the smell that pulled me out of my dream and into reality. Or maybe it had been the smell that had made the dream. It was true either way. That Christmas had been one of the best I'd ever had.

The cinnamon rolls had been perfect, and the pride on my mom's face when I'd taken them into the bedroom had made me happier than any of the gifts under the tree. They'd been great gifts too. A new softball glove to replace the one I'd outgrown with my last growth spurt. Tickets to a Pacers game for Dad and me. A few DVDs I'd wanted.

The scent of cinnamon rolls brought it all back.

I rolled over, letting sleep slough away naturally instead of forcing myself awake. It was Christmas morning, and I wasn't sure if today would be able to top yesterday. It had been the best Christmas Eve I'd experienced since before my mom died. Uncle Anton had done his best to keep the holidays from being awful, and he'd done a great job, but the shadow of what happened had always been there. Last night, however, it had faded behind everything else.

"Good morning." Jalen smiled at me as he brought in a tray of cinnamon rolls. "I figured we could have breakfast in bed."

"If those are any good, we'll make a mess of these thousand-thread-count sheets," I warned him. "Sticky is what makes them good."

His eyes darkened from their normal turquoise to a color halfway between sapphire and emerald. An exquisite shade that turned my insides to mush.

"I think that's a good rule of thumb about anything," he said, his lips curving into a wicked smile.

I laughed as I pushed myself up into a sitting position. He came toward me, and I wasn't sure what made my mouth water more, the food or the sight of him wearing only a pair of low-slung pajama bottoms. I'd taken the matching shirt last night after we'd cleaned up, but he apparently hadn't grabbed another one before heading to the kitchen.

"I'm serious about the sheets," I said as he set down the tray and climbed onto the bed next to me.

He shrugged. "I think I can afford a new set if these are ruined." He cut off a bite of the roll and held the fork out to me. "I can't take credit for making these, but the bakery I got them from is amazing."

I opened my mouth and let him feed me. He was right. They tasted amazing. Ten times better than the frozen ones I'd baked all those years ago, but the taste still made me remember. Except this time, I was able to remember without the grief, and even without the emptiness that sometimes took the place of the sadness. The nostalgia was bittersweet, but I could feel the difference. I wasn't moving on, but I was ready to build a life, and this was one of the steps to doing that.

"What's the schedule for today?" I asked as we shared our breakfast.

"Nothing specific," he said. "My mom and I talked yesterday before I picked you up. She and Armando did a quiet Christmas in Barcelona. Today is all about us. Whatever we want to do."

"Whatever?" I asked, raising an eyebrow.

He made a 'why not' gesture as he finished the bite of cinnamon roll he'd just put into his mouth.

"Can we open presents next?" I asked, aware that my question made me sound more like a child than an adult.

He licked frosting from his lips, a smile curving his mouth. "We can."

"And then make love in front of the fireplace?"

He moved the tray and then rolled over me, pulling me beneath him. "Mind if I amend that to making love in every room? They'll get jealous if we don't."

I slid my hand down his chest, my eyes on his as I moved below the waistband of his pants. My fingers wrapped around his cock, and he sucked in a breath.

"This is a pretty big house," I said, stroking him. His cock swelled under my hand, and I wet my lips. "Are you sure you're up for the challenge?"

He laughed. "Sweetheart, you have no idea how up I am?"

I gave him a not-so-gentle squeeze. "I have a decent idea."

When his mouth came down on mine, I could taste the cinnamon and sugar on his tongue, and I arched up against him. His fingers made their way between my legs, probing and finding me more than ready. Without breaking the kiss, I shoved down his pants and pulled him to me. We groaned as we came together, bodies aligning effortlessly. I was already sensitive from yesterday, and by the end of today, I knew I'd be sore, but I didn't plan on holding back.

We were going to make it a Christmas to remember.

TWENTY-TWO

THEY LAUGHED FROM THE SHADOWS. LURKED AND laughed. Both of them. All of them. They held knives and needles in their hands to cut and poke and hurt and kill.

My hands and feet were free but frozen in place. I stood in the center of the darkness, surrounded by shadows. They reached for me, stabbed me, cut me. My mind flew as drugs invaded my bloodstream, sending me soaring. Even as the world circled around me, I felt every jolt of pain, every tearing muscle.

He ripped me apart, piece by piece, yanking out my insides, breaking my bones. I screamed in agony but made no sound. He was killing me, and I wanted to die. Death would be better than this. Anything would be better than this...

I jerked awake with a gasp of relief. My body throbbed with phantom pain that had, moments ago, been as real as the bedspread under my hands. I fell back against my pillow, concentrating on breathing, letting the nightmare loosen its hold.

It'd been harder than I thought, going back to sleeping alone after the last couple nights. It had been tempting to settle in at Jalen's place, to not ask him to take me home on Christmas night. If I hadn't told Maggie to come into work yesterday, I wasn't sure I would've come back yet. Despite my lack of sleep the last two nights, I knew it'd been the right move. Jalen and I were working toward something serious, something I hoped would one day lead to us living under the same roof, but we weren't there yet.

I still didn't know exactly what drug Serge had given me while I'd been prisoner, but whatever it was had done a number on my sleep cycle. I'd had more nightmares since then than I'd had in a few years. They'd fade again, I knew, but for now, I was done sleeping.

I reached over and turned on the light. It was still early, but I had plenty to do to pass the time. I'd kept up with the basic cleaning since I'd been back, but I hadn't done much in the way of anything else. That seemed like the perfect way to spend a couple hours until the office opened. Some mindless physical exertion to clear my mind.

I'd just gotten out of the shower and dressed after having thoroughly dusted, swept, and scrubbed everything I could think of when someone knocked on my door. I checked the time to make sure I wasn't running behind, but I had a half-hour before Maggie was due.

"Clay, what are you doing here?" I blurted out the question before I realized how it sounded. A gust of wind made me shiver, and I folded my arms to warm myself up. "I mean, come in. It's freezing out there."

"Thank you," he said as he stepped inside. He rubbed his

hands together, then cupped them in front of his mouth and blew on his fingers.

"Want some coffee?" I asked as he bent to take off his boots. "I just made a fresh pot."

"That'd be great, thank you," he said. "Just a spoonful of sugar, if you don't mind."

"I remember," I said with a smile.

The first time Clay had come over to the loft to work on the case that had introduced he and Anton, my uncle had asked me to make them coffee. When Clay had asked for a spoonful of sugar, I'd been unable to resist making a *Mary Poppins* joke. Anton had apologized for me, mortified I'd said something like that to an FBI agent. Clay, however, had just laughed and said that he'd never made the connection. *Mary Poppins* had been his favorite movie when he was four and five years old. He'd worn out his family's copy of it. Anton had harassed him about it every time they had coffee together after that.

I glanced at Clay and saw a reflection of my own nostalgia on his face.

"I miss him too," he said quietly. "He'd be so proud of you, you know."

I shook my head. "Not after what happened at Quantico. There was a lot he and I didn't talk about, but when we did, we were always honest with each other. He would've been ashamed of me for lying."

"We all make mistakes."

I handed him the mug of coffee. "We do."

Our eyes met, and I knew we didn't need to talk about things anymore. What happened was in the past, and it would stay there.

"Not that I'm not glad to see you," I said as I took my coffee to the sofa, "but what brings you here this early?"

"News." He sat down next to me. "The task force the bureau put together raided an auction last night and got their hands on the books for the trafficking ring that had you. Sixteen people were rescued, and we have the names of the people who bought the rest of the group you were with. Warrants went out an hour ago, and arrests are being made as we speak."

I stared at him, unsure if I understood him correctly. "You got them?"

His expression was far too sober for it to be all good news. "We took down six traffickers and twelve potential buyers, including two that matched your descriptions of the scrawny guy and Yerik, but no one named Serge."

I was glad to hear about the rescued people and the arrests made, but the fact that Serge was still out there didn't sit well – obviously. I took a moment to compose myself before saying anything. I didn't want to seem like I didn't appreciate the work the FBI had done. In the whole scheme of things, one kidnapping wasn't at the top of crimes Serge and his men had done.

"That's great, Clay," I said with a half-forced smile. "Hopefully the guys you arrested will be able to point you in the right direction to find Serge."

"The federal prosecutor on the case is already laying out a couple deals for information." He set down his mug. "We already got something out of Yerik though. Not about Serge. About you."

"Me?" I wasn't sure what Yerik could've told the FBI about me that would've been of interest. They already knew

I'd been drugged and beaten. Okay, maybe I said some strange things when I'd been high, but I couldn't think of anything the FBI would want to know.

"When you were mugged a couple weeks ago, it wasn't some random attack."

A chill crept over me. "What do you mean?"

"Yerik told us that one of the other men we'd arrested had been sent by Serge to scare you. Apparently, Serge had thought that if you were mugged while on a case, you'd decide that it was too dangerous to continue working as a PI. And it was some payback too, for rescuing Meka and the other girls."

Oh.

"Serge said his employers weren't happy with me," I said, releasing the tight grip I had on my coffee mug. "I didn't understand at the time. I'd thought that my dad had sent him, but Serge kept acting like he didn't know what I was talking about."

"Serge was the point man for this particular group, which means he has direct contact information for the people above him."

Which meant he'd probably cut a deal. While I would love to see him rot in prison for the rest of his life, I understood the importance of cutting off the head of the snake, and that wasn't Serge.

"You're absolutely sure that one of the men you arrested was the guy who mugged me?"

"He had that personalized keychain of yours on him. He said his name was Ronald, and he'd run out of money partway through the engraving. We managed to convince him that no jury would believe that load of bullshit and that we'd build a kidnapping case against him. He said he was just following orders and told us everything."

I wasn't sure if I felt relieved that I hadn't been subjected to two random violent encounters or worried that the man who'd been responsible for both was still out there.

"We'll get him," Clay said. "I promise."

I nodded. I believed him, but I had a feeling I would never feel completely safe until Serge was found.

TWENTY-THREE

CLAY'S NEWS FROM YESTERDAY SHOULD HAVE KEPT ME on cloud nine for a while, but most of what I'd felt after he left had been numb. I supposed it made sense, not really knowing how to feel after such a sudden change in the case, but when I'd gotten up this morning, I still felt like I was just going through the motions.

Maggie had come in this morning full of her usual bounce and levity, and I'd been tempted to ask her to leave simply because I wasn't sure I could handle her today. Instead, I'd smiled and told her that if no one came in by noon, she could go home. She'd said goodbye less than twenty minutes ago, leaving me alone in the office.

I barely noticed the difference.

I'd made progress on my whiteboard by steadily making my way through a list of every Scott Browne in the area where Salome had sent Helen eight years ago. It wasn't a name as common as John Smith, but it wasn't exactly overly unique either. According to Salome, he was the one whose name went on the birth certificate as the biological father since his partner was half African-American, half-Haitian, and the baby was white. If, by some chance, he and Michael Farmer had split up, the child would've most likely stayed with Browne.

The next one I found was in Nunn, Colorado, not too far from the address Salome had given me. I dialed the number, and after the second ring, a kid answered.

"Hello?"

"Hi, may I speak to Scott Browne, please?"

"Just a minute," the child said politely before yelling, "Dad! Phone!"

This was a landline, I realized with surprise. This probably wasn't the family I needed. I didn't know of anyone under the age of thirty-five who still had a landline. This Scott Browne was probably the little kid's grandfather, not father.

"This is Scott Browne. May I ask who's calling?"

"Hi, my name is June Lewis, and I'm calling from the Foundation for LGTBQ Adoptive Services."

"Uh, I've never heard of them."

The hesitation was small, barely noticeable. I probably wouldn't have even registered it if I hadn't been paying close attention.

"It's a new foundation," I said, working to keep my voice upbeat without sounding overly hopeful. I had to keep up my cover.

Contacting adoptive parents was difficult enough, but I was dealing with an illegal adoption. The parents of Helen's last baby, whoever they were, had to be worried about legal ramifications if they were caught, not to mention the possibility of losing the child they'd raised for the last eight years. I needed to be careful I didn't scare them away.

"Our foundation has been specifically created to assist LGBTQ families looking to adopt, and ones that have already adopted," I continued with the spiel I'd created for this specific task. "Our records show that you inquired about adoption a decade ago, but nothing more recently."

I paused, waiting for him to say what the other Scott Browne's had said. That they didn't have kids. That they hadn't adopted kids. They weren't interested in adoption. They weren't gay.

"My husband and I had been considering adoption, but we ended up going with surrogacy."

I didn't think I imagined the nerves I heard beneath his words. "I would still love to talk to you in person about the ways you and your family could support the foundation."

"But, my daughter is not adopted."

Yeah, my PI's intuition was pinging off the charts. He was on edge.

"That's all right," I said cheerily. "You don't have to be an adoptive family to support the rights of LGBTQ families to adopt."

"Of course, we support – look, send me an envelope with an address where I can send a check. I'm not really interested in doing anything else."

The call ended before I could say another word. Someone else might've chalked it up to Scott simply not wanting to talk to someone he considered a solicitor, but my gut said there was more to it than that.

I needed to go to Nunn and make visual confirmation.

An hour later, I parked across the street from a nice, two-story house. Salome hadn't met Scott or Michael in person or seen a picture, but Scott had provided a few identifying features for Helen, and then Salome had given them to me. They weren't much, but they should be enough to confirm whether I was on the right track.

I planned on waiting for hours, sitting in the car until it was either too dark to see or until someone got suspicious. This wasn't exactly a busy street, so I was guessing it'd be the latter.

To my surprise, however, I hadn't been there more than forty minutes before the front door opened and three people came outside. The little girl wore a hat, but some of her chestnut brown hair had escaped, blowing wildly in the wind.

One of the men had darker skin and a lean, lanky body. I could hear his laugh even though my windows were closed, and the sound of it made me smile. The other man was stocky, probably a good three inches shorter than me, with broad shoulders and a bit of a gut that his bulky coat didn't disguise. His hair was a burnished copper, and he had the sort of fair skin that the sun probably wouldn't be kind to.

All these things matched the description I'd been given of Michael Farmer and Scott Browne, which meant that, unless something was off, these were the people I'd been looking for.

I glanced at my dash. I'd come with the intention to just do visual confirmation, but it hadn't taken as long as I'd planned. It was a risk to make face-to-face contact without having a plan, but I was feeling a bit impulsive.

I waited until Michael took the little girl inside before I got out of the car. Scott had his back to me when I approached, and I shuffled my feet in the snow to let him know I was coming. He looked up from the small section of sidewalk he was clearing when I was only a few feet away and gave a little wave.

"Good afternoon."

"Hi." I gave him a wide smile. "Scott Browne?"

He frowned. "Do I know you?"

"Not exactly." I kept my stance relaxed, my tone easy. "My name's Rona Quick, and I'm a private investigator."

His eyes narrowed. "You're that woman who called about some LGBTQ adoption foundation earlier today."

I held up a hand. "I'm not here for any sort of legal thing. I don't want to make any trouble for you and your family. Please, just hear me out."

He glanced behind him, and I saw his hands tighten on the shovel. "All right."

"Your daughter's biological mother had numerous other children, and one of them hired me to find the others. She just wants to know her brothers and sisters. I promise you, she doesn't want anything that will hurt her sister."

He studied me for a moment, then nodded. "Why don't you come inside so we can talk?"

TWENTY-FOUR

I PULLED INTO THE PARKING SPACE BEHIND MY BUILDING and sat for a moment, my mind still reeling. Danielle Browne was Jenna's half-sister, the one Helen had said was stillborn. The only way to be more certain would be a DNA test, but I didn't think that would be necessary.

Once I sat down with Scott and Michael, I'd been able to show them a picture of Helen, and they confirmed that she had been the woman who sold them their daughter. They also told me that the reason they'd resorted to a black-market adoption had been due to criminal records. In their early twenties, they'd been arrested during an LGBTQ protest, and the prosecutor had wanted to make an example of them. They'd both been convicted of inflated charges and spent six months in prison.

I met Danielle too. She was a beautiful ball of energy with wide brown eyes and a smile that reminded me of Jenna. She'd been thrilled to show me her dance and soccer trophies and to tell me all about the new badge she'd gotten in Girl

Scouts. She'd also explained to me, in that matter-of-fact tone that kids sometimes got when a fact has been presented to them since birth, that she had two dads but no mom even though a mom grew her in her stomach.

I planned on telling Jenna all of this, especially the part where we'd been invited over for a late Sunday brunch where she could meet Danielle, but I knew this was the time when her family usually had dinner, so I decided to wait a bit before calling.

I was halfway up my stairs, thinking about the best way to break the news when the hairs on the back of my neck stood up. The familiar and unpleasant sensation was back, the one that said someone was watching me. I paused and looked around me, trying to make out anything or anyone who was out of place. Despite the cold, people were out walking, enjoying the clear sky and late afternoon sun. No one was paying any attention to me though.

Still, I couldn't shake it.

I hurried up the last few stairs, then dropped my keys as I fished them out of my purse. I cursed as I bent to pick them up, shaking them to knock off the snow. No sooner had I put the keys in the lock than someone spoke behind me.

"I don't want you around the baby."

I nearly fumbled the keys again but managed to catch them between my finger and thumb. "Jalen isn't here, Elise." I gestured toward the parking lot. "You can see his car isn't here, and he doesn't have a key to my place."

"I should hope not."

I'd never actually heard someone feign shock until now, but there was no way Elise was anything but pretending. The expression in her eyes was shrewd, not surprised.

"Anyway, I didn't come here looking for Jalen. I wanted to speak to you."

Great.

I really wished I could be rude and tell her that I didn't want to talk to her, but if I wanted to make this thing with Jalen work, and she was going to have his baby, I needed to at least try to have some sort of polite relationship with Elise. Even if I did despise her.

"Come in," I said as I opened the door. "Can I get you something to drink? I don't have any hot water going, but I can make some coffee or hot chocolate if you want."

"No," she said shortly.

She followed me inside, wrinkling her nose as if my loft smelled like garbage instead of my lavender wax melt. I toed off my shoes and shrugged off my jacket.

"What can I do for you?" I asked, trying not to be annoyed at her rebuffing what had been a sort of peace offering.

"I don't want you around my baby," she said, lifting her chin. "I don't care what you *think* you have with my husband. You're not going to be a part of our lives."

I pressed my lips together and counted to five. "What's between Jalen and me is between Jalen and me. Any issues you have with him, you need to talk to him about."

She shook her head, her perfectly coiffed hair bobbing with the motion. She was a model, so of course, her hair was perfect. Every line of her was elegant, and I wondered how long it would be before she couldn't hide the baby belly.

If she was even pregnant.

I still wasn't entirely convinced. She seemed like the sort

of person who'd stretch the truth if it got her what she wanted, and in this case, what she wanted was Jalen.

"Jalen's a man. He thinks with his cock." She folded her arms. "He likes fucking you now, but he'll get tired of it. He'll come back to me. He always does."

I inhaled slowly, then let the breath out. "Elise, I've had a long day. I know Jalen served you with divorce papers, and I know you won't sign them. That's the only reason you two aren't divorced. He's not getting back together with you."

"He will!" She balled her hands into fists. "We're having a baby, and we're going to be a family!"

Her voice had taken on a shrill edge, but again, I had the feeling she was acting. At least most of it anyway.

"I think you should go," I said calmly. "You've said what you came here to say. Everything else, you can take up with Jalen."

"I think we can handle it between us girls, don't you?" She gave me one of those obnoxious smiles that Queen Bees always have plastered to their faces. The ones that strangers and acquaintances often mistook for friendly, but friends and victims knew were only masks for what lurked beneath.

"There's nothing to handle," I said from between gritted teeth.

The smile dropped away, and she took two steps toward me, one bony finger an inch from poking me. If she did, I wasn't sure I could keep my temper.

"Like hell there isn't," she said. "Let me spell it out for you. Either you stay away from my family, or I will make your life a living hell. I know people who will make sure no one comes near your pathetic little business. I'll run you out of this city if I have to, and no one will stop me."

Enough.

"Out." I walked back to the door and opened it. "Get the hell out, Elise. And if I catch you harassing my customers, I'm calling the cops."

She glared at me as she stormed out, and I barely stopped myself from slamming the door behind her. I'd known she was a piece of work, but to come over here and threaten me like that...I shook my head.

If the baby was really Jalen's, I was going to have to put some serious thought into how I would handle things without killing Elise.

Or I was going to need a good alibi.

TWENTY-FIVE

I BRUSHED THE SNOW OFF THE TOP OF THE TOMBSTONE before setting down the calla lilies I'd brought with me. It was odd, I knew, that I'd never even seen my mother's grave, but I'd been to Adare's more than once. In a way, I almost felt like I could talk to both my mother and Adare here, that Mom would understand why I hadn't been to visit her in Indiana. I supposed that was why I'd brought her favorite flowers today.

"I'll bet the two of you and Anton are up there yelling at me all the time when I do crazy things."

I was the only one here this morning, but I kept my voice quiet, not wanting to disturb the tranquility I'd found. It'd started to snow during the short walk from my car to the gravesite, fat, wet flakes that clung to my clothes and eyelashes and muffled sound. I was reminded of the cemetery scene from *Phantom of the Opera*, the movie with Emmy Rossum and Gerard Butler, not the stage production, and a chill went down my spine.

"Things have been crazy, Adare," I said, running my

fingertips along the edge of the smooth granite. I could feel the cold stone through my glove and pulled my hand back. "I used to think that after what happened when I was a kid, things couldn't get any rougher, but then Anton died. That, I thought, was enough. Now, I've been dealing with human traffickers and kidnappings and finding a child who'd been sold on the black market and being kidnapped myself and the man I love possibly having a baby with the wife who won't divorce him…"

I let my voice trail off as I rambled, my tone rising with each word. All I'd ever wanted was a normal life, or at least as normal a life as an FBI agent could have. The idea of working cases and traveling hadn't been anything I'd considered out of the ordinary. Moving around after I'd gotten kicked out had been different. I'd been restless, unsettled. Then I'd come to Fort Collins and thought I could have a simple life working with Adare. I'd never imagined I'd get caught up in so much chaos here.

Movement behind me made me turn around, my hand automatically going to the coat pocket where I'd put my pepper spray. Fortunately for me, Colorado considered it a defensive item rather than a weapon, which meant it was legal for me to carry. I owned a handgun since my training with the FBI had made me proficient with its use, but I hadn't yet applied for a conceal carry permit and bringing a gun to a cemetery just seemed in bad taste. For a moment, however, as I scanned the area around me for potential threats, I wondered if I'd made the right choice.

"It's just me."

I breathed a sigh of relief as the dark figure heading toward me spoke. "Clay, what are you doing here?"

As he got closer, I saw that he'd bundled himself up well enough that if he hadn't said something, I still wouldn't have been able to recognize him. He waited until he was right in front of me before answering my question.

"I wanted to talk to you."

I raised an eyebrow. "And you couldn't just call? Or come by my place?"

He shrugged. "Things between you and me are okay, but I didn't know how Jalen would react to seeing me. I imagine he's been pretty pissed at me."

"Honestly," I said, "he hasn't mentioned it."

I didn't add that Clay was probably the last person on Jalen's mind right now. Time would eventually smooth things over, and if it didn't, I'd take matters into my own hands. I wasn't going to have the two of them at odds with each other for the rest of our lives.

"Anyway, that's why I came here, where I knew you'd be alone and the chances of Jalen showing up were slim."

My eyes narrowed. "How did you know I was alone? For that matter, how did you know I was here?"

He shifted, as if the question made him uncomfortable. "I've had someone keeping an eye on you since you got out of the hospital. Between your father and Serge, I refused to risk something happening to you again."

That explained why I'd been feeling like someone was watching me. While I was glad it wasn't someone who meant me harm, the idea that Clay had been keeping tabs on me didn't exactly sit well. I wasn't going to argue with him about it here though. I was already getting cold.

"What did you want to talk to me about?" I asked,

rubbing my hands over my upper arms, the friction warming me.

"I wanted to let you know that we arrested two more people involved in the trafficking ring that kidnapped you. They were buyers who had half a dozen people each when we busted them. We think they'll be able to give us some names, and maybe even an idea of where Serge might be."

"You still haven't found him?" I applauded myself for keeping my voice even.

Clay shook his head. "We're turning over every rock we can find, but you know how it is with snakes. They can crawl into places we can't always see."

"Nice analogy," I said dryly.

"Thanks." He stomped his feet. "Can I walk you back to your car, or do you want some more time here?"

"I'm good," I said and looked back at the flowers. "I think Adare would understand that it's cold."

He fell in step next to me, not saying anything until we'd gone a few yards. "We haven't been able to find a trace of your father either."

Right. I didn't only have my kidnapper on the loose, but *him* too.

"Can you think of anywhere he might've gone?"

I shot Clay a surprised look. "It's not like we exchange Christmas cards."

He held up a hand. "I just meant that you might know of somewhere special to your family, somewhere a basic history wouldn't know."

I thought for a minute even though I already knew the answer. I shook my head. "Nowhere. The trips we took weren't particularly nostalgic, at least the ones I can remember. After his accident, he didn't have anywhere special he liked to go. In fact, he preferred to stay inside." I shrugged. "I guess that's something. He'd want to go somewhere he felt safe. Where that is, though, I don't know."

"Thank you," Clay said as he opened my driver's side door. "I'll stay in touch to let you know how things are going."

"Thanks," I said but paused before getting into the car. "Don't be a stranger, all right? I know things are weird right now, but I value your friendship."

I sensed his smile more than saw it.

"I value yours too. Don't worry, Rona, you're not going to lose me."

I sat in the car for a few minutes, letting it warm up as I watched Clay drive away. I really hoped he meant it. I wasn't sure I could handle losing someone else right now.

TWENTY-SIX

"Why didn't you tell me Elise showed up at your place yesterday?" Jenna stared at me from the passenger's seat. "You called me and told me about Danielle but didn't say one word about your boyfriend's pregnant wife threatening to destroy your business. That's the kind of thing you might want to mention to a friend."

I made a dismissive gesture with one hand. "It wasn't important. Not as important as telling you about your sister."

"Bullshit," Jenna said evenly. "I think you didn't want to tell me because you're still in denial over this whole baby thing."

"I'm not in denial," I said, feeling myself bristle. "Elise cheated on Jalen and lied to him multiple times. I think it's actually smart of me to be skeptical about her claim of being pregnant, let alone who the father is."

"Are you going to tell Jalen?" she asked. "He should know that she's threatening you."

"What good's that going to do?" I asked. "She'll deny it,

and then he'll have to decide who he believes. If he says he believes me, it's going to make things tense between the two of them, and if they're going to have a kid together, it'll just make things harder for them, and I don't want to do that."

"Rona."

I heard the warning in her voice and I looked over at her. "It's not just about her. What I do and say will affect Jalen too."

She sighed. "Yeah, you're right. I suppose we can't go tattle to Jalen." She grinned at me. "If she shows up when I'm there, can I slap her?"

"Will Rylan bail you out of jail if she presses charges? Because we both know that if you touch her, she will."

"I'm sure I can convince him."

We made small talk the remainder of the drive, and while she didn't sound nervous, I saw how often she ran her fingers over the scar on the inside of her left arm, the reminder of when she'd tried to take her life as a child. I'd noticed it was something she did whenever she was anxious or talking about something difficult.

"This is a nice house," she said as we pulled into the driveway. "Nice neighborhood too. Not overly rich, but nice."

The curtains over the front window moved, but no one opened the door. I had a feeling Scott and Michael were keeping Danielle inside to give Jenna the time to come to the door herself. I resisted the urge to look behind me to see if I could spot the person Clay had following me. I hadn't told Jenna about that part of my conversation with my friend. She had enough on her mind already.

"Are you ready or do you need a minute?"

"I'm good."

She touched her arm again, but I didn't call her on it. If she said she was ready, she was ready.

We walked up the steps together, and the door opened as we stepped foot on the last one. Scott smiled at us, and behind his back we could see Danielle bouncing on her toes.

"Come in." He stepped out of the way, putting his arm around Danielle, holding her back so we could go inside. "What can I get you to drink? Tea, coffee, cocoa? It's a bit cold out there."

"The cocoa's really good," Danielle piped up, ducking out from under her dad's arm. "Papa makes it himself and puts synonyms in it."

"Cinnamon," Scott corrected.

"Right," she said with a frown. "Synonyms are the words that mean the same thing."

He smiled down at her, then turned to Jenna. "Hi, I'm Scott."

"Jenna." She shook his hand, then took Michael's pro-offered hand.

"Michael."

"And I'm Danielle." She darted forward and wrapped her arms around Jenna's waist. "You're my sister."

Jenna looked startled, but not discomforted by the contact. She hugged the little girl back. "Yes, I am. My name's Jenna."

"That's a pretty name," Danielle said as she grabbed Jenna's hand. "Do you want to see my room? It's purple, and I have a poster of Hope Solo on my wall. She's the best soccer player in the world."

"We still have about fifteen minutes before dinner will be

ready," Michael said. "You're welcome to join me in the living room, or you can go see Danielle's room if you want."

One look at those big brown eyes and there was no doubt in my mind where Jenna was going. With a squeal of delight, Danielle pulled Jenna toward the stairs, leaving me with Michael and Scott.

"I'm happy to help with dinner," I said before the silence could get awkward.

"I've got everything under control, but you're welcome to come into the kitchen and keep me company," Michael said.

Scott and I both followed Michael into the kitchen where the most amazing smells were coming from the stove. The taller man took the lid off a large metal pot and stirred the contents.

"Scott may be the superhero paramedic, but he's useless in the kitchen," Michael said. "Everyone always seems surprised that the mechanic is the cook, but what can I say? My mom taught me well."

"I checked out the website for Burkart Investigations," Scott said as he pulled out a chair for me. "I'm sorry about your partner."

I'd completely forgotten that Maggie had updated the website after Adare's death. "Thank you."

"I hope you don't mind me asking this but was Ms. Burkart your business partner only or..." Michael sounded as concerned as he was curious.

"Mentor and boss," I said with a tight smile. "And a friend, but nothing romantic." I nudged the conversation away from painful thoughts of my friend. "It was my boyfriend who introduced me to Jenna, actually."

"I'm sorry. I'm sure the loss of your friend isn't something you want to talk about," Michael said. "Sometimes my curiosity gets away from me."

"It's okay," I said. "It makes sense that you want to know about me. I showed up in your life out of nowhere. You wanted to make sure I wasn't going to hurt your family."

"We just want to do what's best for Danielle," Scott said.

"That's what Jenna wants too," I assured them.

"Then today, we'll make a toast to a new member of the family," Michael declared. "Two new members. Scott, get out the wine. You know which bottle."

Scott grinned with the slightest hint of an eye roll. "I know which bottle because he always has one pre-selected anytime we have guests 'just in case' we need to make a toast."

I laughed as he moved to a wine cabinet. Some alcohol and relaxing conversation were exactly what I needed.

TWENTY-SEVEN

"You want me to investigate your husband for *what?*" I barely managed to keep the laughter from my voice as I asked for confirmation of what I thought I heard.

Patricia Mauricio was at least eighty-five years-old and looked like my dim memory of Granny Quick, the only one of my grandparents I'd ever known. Pure white hair in tightly rolled curls, lavender cardigan over her floral housedress, horn-rimmed glasses on a silver chain.

"My Gus and I got married in 1950, four days before he shipped out for Korea. Our son, Patrick, was born nine months later," she said, dabbing at her eyes with a monogrammed handkerchief. "We have four children, seven grandchildren, thirteen great-grandchildren, and three great-great-grandchildren. We made it through three years of war and the problems that came home with him. We survived six more years with the army and then the closing of the steel mills back home in Ohio. We've made it through a lot of things that would've torn apart a marriage, but I don't know if we can make it through this."

I opened my mouth, considered what I'd been about to say, then closed it. I liked to think I was a pretty tactful person, but I wasn't sure how to approach my concerns without sounding like I was mocking her. Because I wasn't. It just wasn't the sort of thing I'd expected when she walked in my door fifteen minutes ago.

"Mrs. Mauricio," I began, "you said you suspect your husband of 'committing dietary infidelity.'" I used the same phrase she had.

"That's right." She sniffled and wiped her nose. "It started right after Thanksgiving. I knew something was wrong when he quit taking a second piece of my award-winning blueberry pie, but I thought maybe he was sick or trying to lose weight – heaven knows he has a few more pounds on that spare tire than he should."

"Or maybe he lost his taste for blueberries," I suggested. "I've heard that people's taste buds change as they get older."

She reached across the desk and patted my hand. "You don't understand, dear. Gus and I met at the county fair when I was sixteen and he was seventeen. I had a blueberry pie in the pie contest, and Gus was one of the judges, because of him being the preacher's son. He told me later that he would've voted for my pie even if it hadn't been the best thing he'd ever tasted because no girl would go out with a guy who'd criticized her baking."

"Still," I said gently, "almost seventy years of blueberry pie adds up."

"It's not just the pie," she said, her eyes welling up again. "He'll tell me that he's going to the hardware store for something or to see one of the kids, and when he gets back at lunch or dinner, he says he's not hungry. I've made him all his favorites. Spaghetti and meatballs. Pot roast. Ribs. Lamb chops. All the things he always said he loved."

Okay, that was odd. It didn't necessarily mean that he was cheating on her, but the fact that he was consistently saying he wasn't hungry was concerning, for his health if not for any other reason.

"Then, two days ago, I was making peach cobbler and ran out of sugar, so I went to the store to get some. On my way home, I saw him..." She let out a choked sob. "He was coming out of Taylor Denison's house with a covered plate."

"Did you ask him about it? There could be a perfectly reasonable explanation."

She shook her head, and a plastic curler flew out of her hair and hit the wall. She didn't seem to notice. "I tried. He went straight to the garage when he came home. When I went out there to talk to him, he shoved something into a drawer and said I should knock. I couldn't ask him about it then, but I haven't been able to stop thinking about that covered plate."

"So you think it's this Taylor Denison that he's sleeping with because that's where he's eating?" I asked, latching onto the one part of the story that I could use for an investigation.

She gave me a puzzled look. "Taylor's a man." I was still trying to figure out the best way to tell her that Taylor's gender didn't exactly mean he and Gus weren't having sex when she added, "Gus isn't having *that* sort of affair. We're intimate three or four times a week, and he's an attentive lover."

More information than I needed or wanted, but I kept my expression blank.

"He's having a *food* affair, Ms. Quick, going to his friend Taylor's house and letting that man cook for him. Eating his food." She wiped her eyes again. "I don't know what to do."

"I'll do what I can to help you," I said finally. I had no idea how else I was supposed to respond. I didn't want to take her money, but it was clear she was upset.

"Oh, thank you."

"You're welcome. Now, do you have Taylor's address?" I asked.

She nodded and rattled it off. I jotted it down and then asked the one other thing I needed to know. "Do you know where your husband is?"

I DOUBLE-CHECKED the address before knocking. I was about to have a strange conversation, and I didn't want to repeat it.

The man who answered the door a minute later was tall and wiry, with long jet-black hair and deep wrinkles that made his age impossible to guess. His bronzed skin made me think he had some Native American blood, but he didn't have a trace of an accent when he spoke.

"May I help you?"

"I'm looking for Gus Mauricio. Is he here?"

"Gus!" The man I assumed was Taylor called over his shoulder as he gestured for me to come in. "You have a visitor."

As soon as I stepped inside, I could smell something. It

wasn't unpleasant, but it wasn't familiar either. Meat and spices and something I couldn't put my finger on. It was well past noon, but I wondered if I'd interrupted them at lunch.

A door at the end of the short corridor to my right opened, and a portly man with wisps of gray hair came out.

"Gus Mauricio?" I held out my hand as I stepped forward. He nodded as he gave me a quick shake. "I'm Rona Quick. I'm a private investigator with Burkart Investigations."

"Pats sent you, didn't she?" He looked slightly sheepish, as if he knew exactly what circumstances had led to me being there.

"She did." I'd already planned on being straightforward about this, but the fact that he already knew that his wife had hired me eased some of my anxiety. "Mr. Mauricio, I'll be honest, I really think the best way for me to do what your wife asked is to just come out and ask rather than skulking around trying to figure out what you're doing. She's worried about you not eating at home, and I'd like to be able to go back to her with a reasonable explanation."

He glanced at his friend and nervously ran his hand over what little bit of hair he had. "Venison," he mumbled.

"What was that?"

"We're making venison jerky," he blurted out. "Taylor and me, we got this idea for new spices to add to the venison jerky he makes every year. We're going into business together, and I didn't tell Pats because I knew she'd tell me it was crazy to invest in something like pickled herring flavored jerky, but it's going to be huge. I know it."

For the third time that day, I was speechless.

Fortunately, he kept talking. "We've been experimenting with different flavors which means we have to taste test them.

By the time I go home, I'm so full, I can't eat another bite. Not even Pats' cooking." He grabbed my hand in earnest. "Please, you can't tell Pats. She'll be angry at me for not talking to her about it first."

"I can't keep it from my client," I said. His face fell. "But I can offer to give you until six o'clock tonight to tell her yourself."

I wasn't sure which terrified him more, the thought of me telling his wife or the thought of having to tell her himself, but he agreed to talk to her as soon as he got home. I managed to hold in the laughter until I was safely in my car.

Venison jerky.

Some people.

TWENTY-EIGHT

I closed the Mauricio case after I received a call from a contrite Gus apologizing for taking up my time. He told me they'd mail the check the next day, with a bonus for all the problems they'd caused. I said it wasn't necessary, but he insisted.

I'd already finished my paperwork by the time he called, so after I hung up, I headed home. When the weather got better, I was going to move my things over to the upstairs apartment. I wasn't hurting for money, but there was no point in paying rent if I had a place free and clear, with only property taxes to pay. The thought of being there, living where Adare had lived, no longer freaked me out. In a way, it was almost comforting.

I was rummaging through the fridge for something to eat when someone knocked on my door. After the whole Elise thing two days ago, I wasn't about to open my door without seeing who it was. This time, at least, I was happy to see who was on the other side. Or I was until I opened the door and saw the grim expression on Clay's face.

"What's wrong?" I moved aside to let Clay in.

He didn't sit down, and he didn't take off his coat, which I knew meant whatever had brought him here was even more serious than I'd initially thought.

"Serge is dead."

It took a moment for the words to register, and even then, I didn't quite believe them. "He's dead?"

"I was just down at the morgue," he said as he walked over to one of my front windows and looked out. "FCPD pulled a body from a dumpster behind the Lory Student Center and ran his prints. It came back as our guy."

"When did he...?" I leaned against the table. "How...I don't even know what to ask?"

"They haven't done a full autopsy yet," Clay said, "but whatever the final report says, it's going to be violent and painful."

I opened my mouth to ask for specifics – the asshole had beat and drugged me, after all – but then I took another look at the haunted shadow in Clay's eyes and thought better of it. It had to be bad if it made him look like that.

"Do you think it was rivals or his employers?" I asked. Those mysterious employers that I'd thought might have been my father. Which reminded me, "Any word on my dad?"

"Nothing on any of it," he said. "The FBI took over the investigation, but the chances of it leading anywhere are slim. Serge was a middleman, not important enough to know the big names, but important enough to make problems."

"And my dad?"

"We've gotten in a ton of tips, and we're working with the Indiana cops to follow up on them, but so far, there hasn't been anything solid." His phone buzzed, and he pulled it out of his pocket.

As I watched, his face paled, and he cursed.

"News?"

"Pack a bag." He disappeared into my bedroom.

"Hey, jackass!" I followed. "You don't go into a girl's bedroom without an invitation."

He was at the window when I entered but didn't turn around. "Pack a bag, Rona. I'm serious."

"Yeah, you sound serious," I said, crossing over to stand behind him. "But you haven't given me a good reason why. Or *any* reason, for that matter."

He turned now, and I was surprised to see how shaken he looked. "Our techs just managed to get into the phone we found near the dumpster. Everything points to it being Serge's phone and one of the numbers in it is from DC."

"A lot of people live in DC," I said as his meaning sunk in. "Do we know for sure it belongs to someone in the government?"

"We're still running the numbers, but Ray and I don't want to take any chances. You need to come to Denver with me." He went to my closet and opened it, then stopped. "Where's your suitcase?"

"I'm not going to Denver," I said. "I'm fine here. Just because someone in the government *might* be involved with the trafficking ring that kidnapped me doesn't mean I'm in danger."

"No," he agreed, "it doesn't, but the fact that your license was found next to the phone probably does."

The 'mugging' seemed so long ago that I'd all but forgotten that my license had been taken. My Colorado license. With this address.

"It's possible that Serge could have passed along your information, but even if he didn't, the people who killed him almost definitely have it."

I shoved my hands in my pockets and tried to pretend that the thought didn't chill me to the bone. "If they do, they haven't done anything about it. Why would they wait?"

Clay folded his arms and glowered down at me. "That's not a chance I'm willing to take."

"That's not your choice to make."

"Are you seriously doing this, Rona? I'm just trying to protect you."

I shook my head. "If I'm going somewhere, it's going to be *my* choice. I have a job I love here, and I doubt it'll survive me being gone again for who knows how long."

"You can't be worrying about work when your life is at stake," he argued.

"For someone who works as a profiler, you've been pretty shit with figuring out how I think," I said mildly. "Jalen and I were going to meet in a few hours to go to a New Year's Eve party for his work. I'll stay with him for a few days."

To Clay's credit, he didn't immediately dismiss the idea. He didn't look happy about it, but he at least took a minute to think about it. "All right," he said finally. "Jalen has state-of-the-art security. You'll be safe there too."

"Don't sound so thrilled," I said. "You and Jalen are going to have to get over your issues, you know."

"If he keeps you safe, I'll consider it." He leaned down and picked up a duffel bag. "Now, pack."

TWENTY-NINE

Instead of closing completely, Jalen's company, Sylph Industries, allowed for voluntary work for double overtime on all major religious and federal holidays, as well as a couple days around them for a few minor ones. When I pulled into the parking lot, only a handful of cars remained, though Jalen had told me that almost two-thirds of his employees had come in for half a day. I parked next to Jalen's car and then headed around to the private entrance he'd given me the code for rather than entering the public entrance like I had last time.

My footsteps echoed as I made my way to the elevators. The lights were on, but the lobby still felt dark in that abandoned way that only empty buildings could feel. When I stepped off the elevator, I saw a couple of people scattered through the cubicles and desks, but they barely glanced at me as I made my way to Jalen's office. I had to give them credit for being attentive to their work when most people would've been goofing off.

I knocked on Jalen's door even though it was open, hating to disturb the look of concentration on his face. When he raised his head, however, his smile was one hundred percent genuine.

"I'm almost done," he said, pushing back from his desk and coming around to kiss me. "Sit in here and keep me company while I finish?"

"Gladly." I plopped down on the incredibly comfortable sofa he'd put against the far wall. "It's been a weird day."

"Tell me about it." When I looked at him, he clarified, "Really, tell me about it. I can listen and work at the same time."

"All right," I said, "but remember, you asked for it."

By the time I finished, Jalen had stopped working and given me his full attention. Judging by the dark expression on his face, this was one area where he and Clay, agreed.

"He let you drive over here by yourself?"

I tried not to be offended at the question since I knew it came from a place of concern, but I couldn't quite keep all the bite out of my voice. "No one *let* me do anything. I'm twenty-two and have been on my own since I was nineteen. Plus, I went through FBI training." He opened his mouth, and I held up a finger, knowing what he was going to say. "I know I didn't graduate, but I'm pretty sure the last week didn't have any super-secret-ninja classes I missed."

He stood and came over to where I was sitting. Taking my hands, he crouched down in front of me and kissed my forehead. "You'd be worried about me if some crazies had my name and address, right?"

I sighed and leaned into him. "I just hate feeling helpless."

He smiled and tucked some hair behind my ear. "Helpless is the last word I'd use to describe you."

"Good answer," I said.

He stood, helping me to my feet as he went. "We don't have to go to the party tonight if you're not feeling up to it. People will understand if we stay in and have our own celebration." He wrapped his arms around me, his hands resting on the small of my back. "Champagne, a fire, no clothes..."

"I like the way you think," I said, going up on my toes for a quick kiss. A pleasant shiver went through me at the contact. "But you're the boss. You should at least make an appearance."

"You're more important," he said, brushing the back of his knuckles across my cheek.

The warmth working its way through my body had as much to do with that statement as it did his proximity.

"Let's put in an appearance and see where things go from there," I suggested. "After all, I bought a new dress just for the occasion."

"Did you?" Desire flared up again in his eyes.

"And there might just be a late Christmas present for you under it if you play your cards right."

His mouth crashed onto mine, one hand moving to the back of my head to brace me as his tongue plundered my mouth. Deep, possessing, hot...it was the sort of kiss women swooned over. I wasn't much of a swooner but that didn't stop my knees from going weak.

Only after I was good and thoroughly kissed did he relinquish control. We stood there for a minute, the only sound being our ragged breathing, and I was tempted to ask him to take me right there. If we hadn't needed to go back to my place for me to get the things I'd need for the next few days, I would have done just that, but I wasn't going to inconvenience him anymore than I already was by making him late to his own company's party.

"We should go," I said when I could finally form words. "We have some things to do before the party."

We linked hands as we made our way to the elevator, the tension between us still there, pleasantly simmering below the surface. I could relax with Jalen, feel completely and utterly safe, but I had yet to be around him and *not* want him. Even when he pissed me off, I was drawn to him. I kept waiting for this thing between us to fade and fizzle, but it didn't. If anything, it was hotter and stronger than ever.

"Would you mind leaving your car here?" he asked. "I have an outside company doing security for the lot, and we've never had any issues with people leaving their cars here for a while. There'll actually be a few people leaving their cars here overnight, so they can drink at the party."

"That depends," I teased, "is it some macho thing?"

"I was thinking more along the lines of it being easier for someone to link it to you, but sure, we can go with 'some macho thing.'" He smiled and held open the door for me.

"Mr. Larsen." A prim-looking woman with dark hair and pale skin approached.

"I don't do direct holiday handouts," Jalen said, stepping forward to put himself between her and me. "I have a foundation that handles–"

"She's not here for money," I interrupted. When he looked back at me, I gestured to the stranger. "That's a fifteen-hundred-dollar purse, a two-thousand-dollar jacket, and I don't even want to think about how much those shoes cost if they're what I think they are." At his look of surprise, I added, "How were you married to a model, and you don't know this?"

"That's why I'm here," the woman cut in. "Elise Marx."

That got both of our attention.

"Your friend is right that I don't need, much less want, money from you. My name is Adeline Fowler now, but it used to be Adeline Cornell."

"Any relation to Bernard Cornell?" Jalen asked.

"He's my brother," she said. The hand on her purse tightened. "We're both originally from here. I married an oil man and moved to Texas, but Bernie took over the family business and stayed."

"He's done well," Jalen said. "Last I heard, stock was on the rise."

"Which is, I'm sure, what drew your ex-wife to him," Adeline said, her mouth twisting as if she'd tasted something sour. "He's always spoken highly of you, which is why I came to warn you. Elise came to Bernie about three weeks ago and told him that she was pregnant with his child."

Jalen visibly tensed. I stepped up next to him and put my hand on his arm.

Adeline continued, "He called me because that's what he does when he's in trouble. He told me he'd had a fling with Elise and that they'd used protection, but that it was entirely possible that the child was his. I've met her a time or two at various functions, and I've never liked her. Naturally, I hired someone to look into things for me."

I could practically feel Jalen vibrating with tension.

"My investigator turned up four other men who she'd all told the same thing, including you. They each slept with her over the same two-week period, as did a fifth man, an old boyfriend who doesn't have much in the way of money. I confronted Elise yesterday, and when threatened with a lawsuit, she admitted that the baby is most likely the former boyfriend's. She also told me that if I shared this with anyone else, she'd make me regret it." A tight little smile appeared on Adeline's face. "I've never responded well to threats. And, as I said, Bernie has always liked you, so I decided to make a little side trip before heading to the airport. No one deserves to be blackmailed into a relationship, let alone one with that woman. Happy New Year, Mr. Larsen."

THIRTY

WHEN JALEN FIRST TOLD ME ABOUT THE NEW YEAR'S Eve party he wanted us to go to, I'd planned on buying a new dress for the occasion even though he said there wasn't any specific dress requirement. The lingerie, however, had been more of an impulse buy while I'd been out, something I'd seen and immediately known Jalen would love.

Sheer black thigh-high stockings connected to black garters. A tiny bra and panties that barely covered anything. The fabric slid like liquid silk against my skin, every movement sensual. My nipples hardened, and I knew that by the end of the night, my panties were going to be soaked.

The dress was simple, a midnight blue that bordered on black. Three-quarter sleeves and a mid-calf hem, a neckline that kept my scar from being visible. It was brushed velvet, and I kept running my hands over it, enjoying it almost as much as my underthings. I'd never been a huge fan of dresses, but this one was surprisingly comfortable.

And it didn't hurt to have Jalen looking at me with that gob-smacked expression on his face either.

"Are you sure you want to go?" He traced my bottom lip with the tip of a finger. "I think we could find something else to occupy our time."

"As tempting as the offer is, we need to go for at least an hour." I kissed his cheek. "Do you think you can wait that long?"

His eyes narrowed, and he caught my chin. "I'll do my best, but no promises." He kissed me, brief but hard, then stepped back, the heat in his eyes making me want to reconsider my position.

The party was in full swing when we arrived even though it had technically only begun a half hour ago. Jalen had gone all out with a live band, open bar, and tables packed with all sorts of food. Not that pretentious stuff most rich people ate, but not that cheap shit that companies generally pawned off on their employees.

And I was pretty sure that was a chocolate fountain.

"Are you okay?"

"Hmm?" I looked up at Jalen.

"You have this weird look on your face," he said, leaning down so I could hear him. "Is everything okay?"

I pointed. "You got a chocolate fountain."

He shrugged. "I can't take the credit. My assistant did the planning."

"Two words," I said after licking my lips, "*big bonus*."

He laughed, the skin at the corners of his eyes crinkling. He'd have laugh lines there when he got older, but I pictured it in my head, him as a middle-aged man. Wrinkles around his eyes and mouth, some silver in his dark hair.

He'd be like Harrison Ford, hotter than hell no matter what age.

And, based on the way most of the women were looking at him, I wasn't the only one who thought that way.

"I feel like dancing," I said, surprising myself. "Do you feel like dancing?"

"I'm not really much of a dancer," he said.

I smiled up at him and took both of his hands, walking backward to pull him with me onto the dance floor. "We have reason to celebrate."

He put his hands on my hips, and I put mine on his shoulders, then I followed him as he took a few steps. We kept some space between us, aware of the eyes on us, but the distance did nothing to dissipate the energy surrounding us. I felt like a huge weight had lifted off my shoulders, and the ease with which Jalen was moving made me think that he felt the same.

A part of me wanted to ask him if he was as relieved as I was that he wasn't going to be a father, but another part of me wasn't sure I wanted to know the answer. We hadn't talked about kids. Hell, we hadn't talked about the future much at all. Everything between us had been so punctuated by the craziness that there'd never seemed a good time for the serious things.

And I hadn't been ready for the serious things.

Now, I thought I was, but I didn't know if he was, and I didn't want to force it. I didn't want to risk losing him if he didn't want the same things I wanted. Like kids. I wanted kids. More than one so they'd have each other. But what if he didn't want kids? What if the reason he looked so relieved was because he never wanted kids at all?

He buried his hands in my hair, the rough touch pulling me out of my own head. His eyes were blazing as he kissed me, his teeth worrying at my bottom lip until everything else faded and all I was aware of was the feel and taste and smell of him.

A wolf whistle cut through the music and the haze, and we broke apart. Before I could step away, he grabbed my hips and pulled me to him. The smile on his face was a new one, and it took me a moment to place it.

Joy.

Real, genuine joy. Also, happiness and love and desire, all without a trace of shadow.

I wanted to see that look on his face more often. All the time.

I pulled his head down, but not for a kiss. I put my lips against his ear and whispered, "Let's go home. I want to show you what I'm wearing under this dress."

THIRTY-ONE

"You were wearing *that* under your dress?"

I did a slow turn, letting him see the whole thing. By the time I was facing him again, he'd removed his shirt and had taken two steps in my direction. I reached behind me to unhook my bra, but a hoarse command stopped me.

"Leave it."

I dropped my hands and waited for his next instruction.

"Sit."

I sat on the edge of the bed, and he went to his knees. The hands that skimmed my calves up to my thighs were hot, but it only added to the fire already burning my skin. My pulse raced as he pressed his lips to the side of first one knee, then the other. He took his time trailing tickling kisses up my thighs, then across my stomach and up to my breasts. He gripped my waist as he latched onto a nipple through my bra, and I cried out as a jolt of electricity went straight south. I squirmed, the suction and pressure nearly too much, but he held me tight, took me right to the edge.

"Fuck," I groaned, digging my hands into his hair.

"Soon," he said with a smile. "I fully intend to make you come this year and next."

My nails scratched his scalp as he turned his attention to my other breast. He worried at the tip with his teeth, the sensation intensifying until I wasn't sure I could handle any more. Unable to articulate what I was feeling, I tugged on his hair until he raised his head.

Wickedness gleamed in his eyes as he stood. "Do you remember your safe word?"

I nodded, everything in me clenching in anticipation.

"Up on the bed." Once I obeyed, he followed and pulled off his belt. "Let's get those hands out of my way."

Less than two minutes later, my hands were tied together and lashed to the headboard as I knelt facing the back wall.

"Now what?" I asked.

"Now I get back to where I was before I was so rudely interrupted."

I almost asked what he meant, but then I didn't need to because he was under me and pulling me down until he could run his tongue along the already-wet fabric.

"Shit," I gasped.

He didn't say anything, but his tongue was busy. It caressed my skin, slipped between my lips, danced over the abundance of nerves that throbbed and pulsed under the oral assault. I came once with a shudder, but he didn't stop. I closed my eyes, my hips moving in short jerks as another wave of pleasure rolled over me. As if from far away, I heard soft whimpering sounds that, on some level, I understood I was making, but I couldn't stop myself.

"Had enough?"

"J..." I grabbed onto the headboard.

"One more, sweetheart."

I shook my head but didn't say the word I knew would stop him. My muscles trembled, and I wanted to tell him that it wasn't going to happen, but if I'd learned anything during the time I'd known him, it was that he could do anything he put his mind to.

I cursed as I came again in an explosion of ecstasy and color. For a moment, I thought the latter was in my head, but then I heard loud pops that my brain registered as fireworks in the distance.

"Happy New Year," Jalen said breathlessly as he moved from underneath me to behind me. He leaned over and kissed my shoulder. "Ready to help me ring it in properly?"

THIRTY-TWO

"ALL RIGHT," I SAID AS I SET MY PLATE ASIDE. "YOUR turn. What was your worst New Year's resolution?"

"That's not fair," Jalen protested. "You didn't answer my question."

"I did," I countered. "I can't help it if you didn't like my answer."

"You can't really expect me to believe that you've never broken a New Year's resolution."

I grinned at him. "It's not hard when you don't make them in the first place."

His eyes narrowed, and he rolled over me, bracing himself on his elbows so that his body was a comfortable weight on mine rather than suffocating.

"I make you breakfast in bed, and you take advantage of my trusting nature?" He kissed my chin. "I think I'm going to need to punish you for that."

I reached up and linked my fingers together behind his neck. "Did you have something particular in mind?"

The hot length of him hardened against my leg, and I shifted, eager to have him inside me again despite the twinges and aches from our previous activities. We'd made love until we'd both passed out from exhaustion and our skins bore the evidence of our passion in teeth and nail marks. I'd also spotted a few bruises on my hips and on Jalen's arms from where we'd gripped each other too hard.

"I have a lot of things in mind," he said, his knee pressing between my legs. "But for right now, I just want to be buried in that hot, wet cunt of yours."

The doorbell rang, ruining the mood.

"Dammit," Jalen growled. "Maybe if we ignore them, they'll go away."

The bell rang three more times in quick succession.

"I'm thinking not," I said with a sigh.

Two more rings.

"Oh, for fuck's sake!" Jalen rolled off me and onto his feet in one smooth motion. I had a moment to appreciate his firm ass before he yanked on a pair of jeans. "Stay here. I'll be right back."

I reached over to the bedside table and snatched the last bite of his chocolate chip muffin. Desertion resulted in the forfeiture of all delicious breakfast rights, I decided. Besides, he was already going to torture me. I might as well have made it worthwhile.

I was still deciding whether I wanted to play contrite or rebellious when raised voices came from downstairs.

"Get out of my way, Jalen!"

Shit. Elise.

I grabbed one of Jalen's shirts and a pair of his boxers, pulling them on as quickly as possible.

"Not today, Elise," Jalen said. His voice was even, but I knew he was pissed. "We're going to talk, but not today."

"Is she here? Is that why you want me to leave? That home-wrecking slut is here."

I stepped into the front room just as she finished. "Present."

"You don't need to be down here for this," Jalen said. "Elise was just leaving."

"Like hell I am," she snapped. "This is my house!"

"No, Elise," he shot back. "This is *my home*. You may have lived here on and off when we were together, but we both know you didn't contribute a single penny to it."

"Because I had to keep places in New York and LA since you wouldn't move to either city!"

She took a step toward him, and I took a good look at her for the first time. Her hair barely looked brushed, and her clothes were wrinkled. Her cheeks were flushed, and her mascara smudged.

"You're trespassing," Jalen said, folding his arms over his chest. "Don't make me call the police. You know it'll end up in the tabloids, and neither of us want that."

"You won't do it. You won't have the mother of your child arrested simply for wanting to talk to you."

I made a derisive sound that drew her glare to me. "We know he's not the father of your baby. If you're even pregnant at all."

"I am pregnant, you bitch! How dare you accuse me of lying!"

I lifted a shoulder. "Well, you're a liar, so there's that," I said mildly.

"A woman named Adeline Fowler came to see me yesterday," Jalen said, his voice surprisingly calm and low. "She claims that you told her brother that he was the father."

Elise jutted out her chin like some mutinous child. "She's lying."

"So you do know her?" I asked.

Elise flushed an even deeper shade of red. "I've seen her at various events. She's always been jealous of me."

"I'm supposed to believe that it's a coincidence that the day after I'm told you're telling multiple men that you're pregnant with their kid, you show up here, demanding we talk?"

"I want us to be a family." Tears glittered in her eyes.

Crocodile tears.

"Maybe you can explain something to me, then," he said. "I dropped my phone in the living room on Monday, and it bounced under the couch. Imagine my surprise when I found it and a pack of condoms beneath it. One was missing."

Elise shrugged but didn't meet Jalen's eyes. "How am I supposed to know where you fuck her?"

A muscle in his jaw twitched. "The receipt was down there too. It was from that night. We used a condom."

"You don't know that," she countered. "It doesn't mean anything. And they don't always work. It says so right on the package."

"If you're that sure, go to the doctor tomorrow and get a paternity test," I suggested. "Then we'll all know for sure."

"*I* know for sure," she snapped. "And you stay out of this. I told you that I don't want you anywhere near my baby or my husband."

"Give it a rest, Elise." Jalen shook his head.

The doorbell rang again.

"What the hell?" I muttered as I moved to get it. "What's the point of having state-of-the-art security if people can get to the damn door?"

I opened the door and thought of a better question.

What was the point of having a camera to show who was outside the door if no one used it?

"Happy New Year, little girl," my father said. "It's time for me to finish the job."

THIRTY-THREE

I GRABBED THE DOOR AND TRIED TO SLAM IT SHUT, BUT my shock had lost me a second, and I wasn't fast enough. He slapped his hand against the door and shoved, knocking me back. I would've fallen if he hadn't reached out and grabbed the front of my shirt. Jalen's shirt.

"Not a word," my father hissed as he yanked me forward.

Cold steel slid along the side of my neck, and I braced myself for pain. I'd die without a sound if it meant keeping Jalen safe.

"Don't walk away from me!"

Elise's shrill voice destroyed any hope I'd had that Willis would kill me and go before he realized we weren't alone.

"Rona is–" Jalen's question dropped away as he stepped into view. "If you hurt her, I'll kill you."

Willis spun me around, holding me in front of him like a shield. "I remember you from my trial. You were there for the whore."

Jalen's hands curled into fists, but his eyes found mine. "It's going to be okay."

"Who else is here?" My dad demanded.

"No one," Jalen said quickly.

"I'm 'no one' now?"

Not quick enough.

Elise stomped out of the living room and skidded to a stop as she saw what was happening. She held up her hands and took a step backward.

"Stop!" Willis pointed his knife at her. "I came here to finish my job. Let me do that, and you get to live."

"Jalen?"

"Do what he says."

My brain scrambled to find a way out of this situation. I knew this. At Quantico, we'd gone over the different sorts of moves to make when being held from behind. Flip him over my back? Smash his instep? An elbow to the solar plexus? I couldn't remember what we'd been told to do if our captor had a knife. Any movement felt like it'd be my last.

"Don't hurt me," Elise pleaded. She put her hands on her stomach. "I'm pregnant. Please don't hurt me or my baby."

My father hadn't cared about killing his own wife and unborn child. A stranger and her baby wouldn't move him. I didn't tell Elise that though. As much as I despised her, this wasn't something I'd wish on anyone.

"Who's the father?" Willis asked.

"He is," Elise said immediately, pointing at Jalen.

"I'm not," Jalen said, taking a step toward me. "They have nothing to do with me."

"You're really going to deny it now?" Elise wailed. The

tears spilling down her cheeks now were probably real. "All you care about is *her*!"

I could've told her that Jalen was trying to protect her and the baby by making Willis think that they wouldn't be leverage, but every time I swallowed, I felt the sting of the knife's blade. Talking wouldn't be the smartest thing to do right now.

"She's trying to make you think her bastard is yours?"

The air in the room shifted with the question. Elise and Jalen looked confused, but I knew exactly what had changed. My father was identifying with Jalen now, not as a potential threat, but as an ally.

"My cheating bitch of a wife tried to do that to me too."

The knife at my throat moved slightly as Willis adjusted his grip on me. Instead of it being positioned so that he could cut my throat straight across without needing to apply much pressure, it was at an angle and now half an inch from my skin. The slight flick of Jalen's gaze told me that he'd seen it too. It wasn't much, but it was more than I'd had a minute ago.

"After I'm rid of this slut, you can do that one, and then we can get a drink before we take care of the bodies. That's what went wrong last time. I didn't get the chance to get rid of the evidence."

The casual way my father spoke of murder and body disposal was more chilling than the shouting and ranting.

"Can I take care of her too?" Jalen asked, his expression a mask of calm. "I mean, she's not pregnant, but she's been a lot of trouble."

"Do you think I'm an idiot?!" Willis shouted. "You're going to kill them and blame it on me!"

I felt his muscles tense a split second before he moved,

and I acted on instinct, spinning toward the knife rather than away from it. I jerked my head down and away as I dropped to my knees and rolled, ignoring the agony ripping across my jaw and up my cheek. I couldn't tell how bad the damage was as hot liquid spilled down my face, but I could see and breathe, and that was enough.

Everything seemed to happen all at once.

Jalen shouted my name.

Willis cursed and kicked at me.

Elise screamed and covered her stomach.

She really was pregnant.

The realization hit me a moment before I knew what my father was going to do next.

I reached out and grabbed his foot, the sickest feeling of déjà vu coming over me. He twisted as he fell, and for a moment, his eyes met mine. Something that looked a lot like relief flashed across his face, and then he slammed into the floor. The world went still, as if everything held its breath to see what would happen next.

He didn't move.

Jalen knelt, putting himself between me and Willis. Cautiously, he reached down, fingers pressing against my father's neck. When he turned toward me, I knew it was over. I closed my eyes and let Jalen wrap his arms around me as he shouted at Elise to stop freaking out and call the police. I might cry later, but right now, I was just glad that it was done.

THIRTY-FOUR

"THAT'S ONE HELL OF A WAY TO START THE NEW YEAR."

"Clay!" I tried to get up, but a glare from Jalen kept me seated. He'd been fussing over me the whole time, and I knew it'd eventually get annoying, but right now, it was endearing.

My friend was pale as he came over to me and pulled me into a hug. To my surprise, Jalen didn't say a word. When Clay finally pulled away, he held out a hand to my boyfriend.

"I was an ass."

"Yes, you were," Jalen agreed, but he shook Clay's hand.

"Glad to see you two are safe," Agent Matthews said as he came into the room. "Are you feeling up to giving your statements?"

"Can't it wait?" Jalen asked. "She's had a rough morning."

"It's okay," I said. "My face is still numb, and I'd rather do it before the medicine wears off, and it hurts to talk."

The cut I'd received wasn't too deep, but it ran from my chin, across my cheek, ending just below the corner of my right eye. Jalen had insisted on a plastic surgeon being called in to take care of it, and I'd been told it probably wouldn't scar, or at least not badly. Oddly enough, I wasn't concerned. The people I loved wouldn't reject me because of a new scar, and that was the only thing that mattered to me.

"I gave my statement to the officers out there," Jalen said.

"The doctor kicked him out because he yelled at her when I winced during the assessment," I said with a half-smile.

"I apologized," he said as he reached for my hand.

"Just tell us in your own words what happened." Agent Matthews sounded amused by the exchange.

I took a moment to gather my thoughts. I wanted to be thorough but as unemotional as possible. What I'd done should have been cut-and-dry, but if I wasn't clear about anything, I could end up in trouble.

"Jalen and I were in bed when the doorbell rang. He went downstairs to see who it was." It wasn't any easier to tell it than it had been to live it. I squeezed Jalen's hand tighter with each minute. When I finally reached the end, my body shook, but my voice was steady. "That's when we called for an ambulance."

"Shit, Rona." Clay put his hand on my shoulder. "You shouldn't have had to do that. We should've caught him before he got to you."

"Yes, you should have," Jalen said.

"J," I warned.

"What about your security?" Clay asked Jalen. "The whole reason I agreed to let Rona stay with you was because I thought you could keep her safe."

"Hold up." I stuck my hand between the two of them. "If

the two of you keep talking about me like I'm not here, you're both going to need a doctor to reattach your balls. Got it?"

Jalen raised an eyebrow. "I thought you liked my balls where they were."

I scowled a warning. "I like being treated like a person more."

He leaned over and kissed my forehead. "I'm sorry. You should be the one to yell at Clay."

"I'm not going to yell at either one of you," I said. "Everyone's made mistakes. We're not going to debate who did or didn't do worse."

They were both silent for a moment, then nodded.

"I'll be meeting with my security people to see what went wrong," Jalen said. "Just because your father's not a danger anymore doesn't mean you're safe. There's still whoever killed Serge."

"Actually, there's not," Agent Matthews interjected as he came into the room. "Part of the reason we think your father was able to get past us was because we had to pull men off looking for Willis to help with the trafficking case. We caught a huge break."

Clay picked up from there. "The coroner found a brand on Serge's body, made post-mortem. Turns out, it was a signature used by his killer. We were able to use it to connect him to other murders, and after that, things fell into place. Dozens of our agents are out there right now, making arrests, conducting raids. The men we arrested before are making as many deals as they can. No one has anything to gain by coming after you."

"Obviously, we're going to encourage you to lay low for a

couple weeks until we finish cleaning things up," Agent Matthews said. "Do you have somewhere you can do that?"

"I think I can find somewhere," Jalen said. "Are we allowed to leave the area?"

"Even Elise is saying you didn't intend to kill him," Agent Matthews said to me. "Actually, she said you were trying to stop him from hurting her and her baby."

Clay looked at me with surprise. "You saved *Elise*?"

"I wasn't going to let him hurt anyone else," I said softly. "No matter how much she pisses me off."

"Oh, I almost forgot." Agent Matthews reached into his pocket and pulled out a piece of paper. "She gave me this to give to you, Jalen. I'm guessing it means something to you."

Jalen took the paper, read it, then smiled. "It's the official conception window. A week *before* I slept with her. The baby can't be mine."

Relief washed through me. Adeline's visit had made me certain that Jalen wasn't the baby's father, but this meant we were done with Elise's games.

"She wrote a note on it too," he said. *"You were right. We used a condom. I'll sign the papers."*

"No apology," I said with a shrug. "But on the plus side, you're going to get a divorce."

"I didn't want to get it this way," Jalen said.

For the first time, I heard something new in his voice. Something hard. And I wasn't the only one who heard it.

"We're going to talk to the cops," Agent Matthews said. "And then we've got paperwork piling up back at the office. We're going to be busy for a while with this case."

Clay leaned over and gave me a quick hug. "If you need me, all you have to do is call."

I nodded. "I know." I waited until they left before I asked Jalen what was wrong.

He stared at me. "You could've died today. Why did you risk yourself for Elise? Dammit, Rona!"

"Are you mad at me for saving her life? Really?"

He cupped my face in his hands, careful to keep his fingers off my wound. "I can't lose you. Don't you understand that yet? Losing you would kill me."

I curled my fingers in his shirt. "And I couldn't have lived with myself if he hurt someone else when I could've stopped him."

Jalen rested his forehead on mine. "Please, sweetheart, don't ever scare me like that again."

"*Ever?*" I echoed. "That sounds an awful lot like a commitment."

He smiled. "One step at a time, right?"

I wanted to enjoy this moment, but there was one thing I had to know before I could. "When you heard Elise was pregnant, was it the baby you didn't want, or was it just her?"

He raised his head but didn't step away. "You want to know if I want kids?"

I nodded.

His eyes skimmed down to my belly. "Are you—"

"No, but if we're looking to the future, it's something we should talk about."

He smiled and kissed the tip of my nose. "I want to be a father someday, but only if you're the mother."

I closed my eyes and finally let myself feel all the hope I'd been pushing down for so long. I was going to have a family.

No, I amended. I already *had* a family. It was just going to get bigger someday.

THIRTY-FIVE

"You do realize that you're certifiable, right?" I said as I joined Jenna next to the pool. "Feeding this many people."

Jenna grinned at me. "It's all in the delegation."

We both looked over at the grill where Rylan and Zeke were busy with an insane amount of meat. Nearby was a long table weighed down with chips and dips, potato salad, scalloped potatoes, fruit salad, cheese, crackers, cold cuts, buns, fresh vegetables, pies, brownies, Jell-O, condiments, and about half a dozen other dishes that I couldn't recognize from my seat.

"Mom look!" Diana called from the pool. "Look what Aunt Stacey taught me!"

When she was sure we were watching, she flipped onto her back and floated. Less than an arm's length away was Stacey, hand out to help if Diana faltered. While both of Jenna's sisters had met the family back in March at Diana's birthday party, Stacey had been coming by twice a week since school had let out last month. Both kids got along with her, but Diana had become obsessed. Everything was all about her Aunt Stacey.

"That's great," Jenna said with a sincere smile.

"I'm surprised Jeremiah's not in there with them," I said.

"He and Danielle are in a serious competition at the moment." Jenna gestured toward the driveway. "They're playing Antelope."

"Antelope?"

She laughed. "Apparently, spelling *horse* wasn't enough of a challenge."

"Let me guess, that was Danielle's doing." Scott took the seat on the other side of Jenna while Michael sat down at the edge of the pool and dangled his feet in the water. "She's become obsessed with going to the national spelling bee next year. She's becoming extremely competitive."

"I wonder who she gets that from," Michael said dryly.

As the two men continued to banter, I found my gaze wandering. Suzette was sunbathing a couple chairs away and judging by the looks her brother and Zeke were throwing at her, she was going to end up getting wet, soon. I knew Zeke's new boyfriend was around here somewhere too, as were Stacey's parents. The Johnsons had been a little more reluctant to join a family holiday, but Jenna had managed to convince them that they wouldn't feel out of place. Things between them and her were much better as time went on.

The only person missing was Clay, but it wasn't because something was wrong. In fact, I'd talked to him a couple days ago, and he was doing better than he had been in a long time. He'd promised that he'd come by as soon as he returned to Colorado, which should be soon.

The hairs on the back of my neck stood up, and I felt the familiar sensation of being watched. It wasn't, however, an unpleasant one. I turned toward it and found Jalen staring at me, heat in his eyes. I'd had a couple cases I'd needed to finish up before the holiday, so it'd been several days since the two of us had done anything more than texted and talked for a few minutes.

When he'd picked me up, the kiss he'd given me had made me want to stay in for the night, but we'd already promised Jenna we'd come to her Fourth of July picnic, and we'd been running late. I didn't plan on doing anything to prevent today from being perfect for my friend, but I was already eagerly anticipating all the decadent things he'd promised me on the way here.

I STOOD at the foot of the bed and took a moment to admire my work.

Jalen sat with his back against the headboard, his arms stretched out along the top with each wrist tied to a post. I'd put the blindfold on him first, knowing from my own personal experience that it would heighten the experience. Then I'd undressed him, restrained him, and left him waiting, stark naked and looking gorgeous.

I climbed onto the bed, keeping my eyes on him as I inched closer. I put my hands on his ankles and slid my palms up as I went. The hair on his legs was coarse against my palms, and his muscles flexed beneath his skin. I loved his body. He was magnificent. The sort of man whose physique deserved to be made from stone and admired in a museum somewhere. But also the sort of man who would dismiss such a statement as completely ludicrous. He knew he was attractive, but I doubted he understood the extent. In my opinion, that made him even more incredible.

By the time I stopped, his cock was thick and full, curving up toward his stomach and I knew that when I took it in hand, it would be heavy, both soft and hard at the same time.

He was like that too. Soft and hard at the same time.

"Are you going to stare at it all night or what?"

"You should be more patient," I said as I stretched out between his legs.

"I am being patient," he argued.

I wrapped my hand around the base of his shaft, and he let out a low oath. My tongue teased the tip, and his head fell back, hitting the wall with a thunk. I didn't often have him at my mercy, and I intended to take advantage of the opportunity. He moaned as I slowly fisted his cock, using my tongue to ease the friction of skin on skin. His hips jerked, and I stopped, tightening my hold until he stopped moving.

"Wait until it's my turn," he warned.

My pussy clenched in anticipation, and this time it was my own impatience I had to reign in. I shifted to get a better grip on the base of his shaft and then finally gave him what he wanted. Leaning down, I wrapped my lips around the head of his cock. Sucking hard, I took more of him into my mouth, an inch at a time until he couldn't go any deeper.

"Fuck..." he groaned. The muscles in his thigh jumped and bunched under the hand I was using to steady me. "Your mouth is going to kill me."

I didn't answer, keeping my attention focused on the delightful bit of flesh in my mouth. I'd once heard somewhere that when the taste of another person's body – their skin and saliva and sweat and... other things – was appealing, it meant that they were your soulmate. Like it was nature's way of ensuring that the people who'd make the strongest and best offspring would want to be together. If that was the case, then Jalen and I were meant to be. I couldn't get enough of him.

My tongue traced the pulsing vein on the underside of his cock, then circled the tip, gathering up the drop of pre-cum beaded there. I dropped my hand from his thigh, reaching down to cup his balls. I rolled them in my hand, alternating a gentle touch with a rougher squeeze.

Jalen pulled on his restraints, muttering a combination of curses and filthy promises, only half of which made any sense at all. I'd set out to drive him crazy, and it looked like he was there. Not a moment too soon either because if I had to wait any longer to feel him inside me, I knew I'd go crazy.

I lifted my head, dragging my teeth along his sensitive skin until he was begging me to stop. We'd long-since established safe words, and since nothing he said truly meant slow down or stop, I kept going. By the time I released his cock, he was simply repeating *fuck* over and over.

I kissed my way up his chest, pausing at his nipple to tease it with teeth and tongue. When I switched to the other one, I moved my knees to either side of his hips. His cock brushed against the inside of my thighs, and he caught his breath. I put my hands on his shoulders for balance and kissed him. His tongue tangled with mine as he tried to take control of the kiss, but I didn't let him. He'd be in charge later. Right now, it was my turn.

I whimpered as I lowered myself onto his slick cock. I was wetter than I'd ever been, but he was thick enough that coming together was a tight fit. My body stretched to accommodate his size, and his dick rubbed against my walls with the perfect amount of friction. I let out a shaky breath when he was finally all inside. It didn't matter how many times we'd done this, it still amazed me how perfectly we fit together.

"Take off the blindfold," he said, his voice strained. "Please, Rona, I want to see you."

I kissed him as I rolled my hips, sinking my teeth into his bottom lip when the movement sent a ripple of pleasure through me. He tugged against the soft leather cuffs that kept his wrists bound, then chased after my mouth when I broke the kiss. He made a sound of pure frustration, and I let him growl for a few more seconds before I granted his request and removed the blindfold.

He blinked against the dim light, then zeroed in on my face. "Hands. I want my hands."

I ran my fingers through his hair and rolled my hips again. He cursed, and I smiled. "What do I get if I let you go?"

His eyes narrowed. "I'm going to fuck you so hard you'll feel it for days."

I tilted my head, pretending to think as I rose up on my knees, then slid back down on him. "I don't know. I'm enjoying fucking you. I think I need a little more incentive than that."

He gritted his teeth. "How about I wake you up every morning for a month using my mouth?"

I paused just as I'd pushed up onto my knees again. "Every morning for a month? How, exactly, is that going to work for the days I'm at my place?"

"I figured maybe you wouldn't go back to your place."

He gave me a rakish grin, but I could see something else in his eyes. Something that told me he wasn't completely joking.

"Are you...are you asking me to move in with you?"

"I am."

I held his gaze for a moment, then reached over to undo his right wrist. He undid the left one himself as I shifted my legs to wrap around his waist. His arms locked around me as he claimed my mouth.

The world became heat and skin and teeth, waves of pleasure that threatened to overwhelm. The scent of him surrounded me, infused itself into every cell. He placed a hand on the small of my back, guiding me as we moved together.

"I'm not going to last long," he murmured against my mouth. "Touch yourself. Let me watch you come first."

I leaned back, trusting him to hold me up as I dropped my hand between us. My fingers found my clit swollen and throbbing. Quick, rough strokes pushed me closer to climax, but it wasn't until he sank his teeth into my breast that I came with a cry.

I rode my high as he drove up into me with hard, deep strokes. Once, twice, and then he was saying my name, his cock pulsing inside me. A shudder ran through him, the motion sending another ripple of pleasure through me. We stayed locked together as we came down in a post-orgasmic haze. Only as the air conditioning cooled our heated skin did we finally move.

Once we were under the covers, limbs tangled, I asked, "Were you serious? About me moving in?"

"I meant to ask you with some romantic gesture," he

admitted, "but I don't always think clearly when I'm tied up and horny."

I laughed and snuggled closer. "Good. I was hoping it wasn't some heat of the moment thing."

"Does that mean you're saying yes?"

I nodded and looked up at him. "I am. On one condition."

"What's that?"

"You've got to let me get rid of that hideous end table in the living room. I'm constantly running into those awful clawed feet."

He laughed and kissed my forehead. "Love, you can redecorate the entire house if you want. The only thing I care about is falling asleep next to you every night and waking up next to you every morning."

"Good answer," I said, closing my eyes.

My body relaxed against his, and I felt sleep sneaking up on me. That was okay though. We'd work out the details tomorrow. Or the day after.

We had time.

THE END

Hope you enjoyed the New Pleasure series. Stay tuned for Clay's story coming in October.

Dom X Box Set

Unlawful Attraction Box Set

Chasing Perfection Box Set

Blindfold Box Set

Club Prive Box Set

The Pleasure Series Box Set

Exotic Desires Box Set

Casual Encounter Box Set

Sinful Desires Box Set

Twisted Affair Box Set

Serving HIM Box Set

Pure Lust Box Set

ABOUT THE AUTHOR

M. S. Parker is a USA Today Bestselling author and the author of over fifty spicy romance series and novels.

Living part-time in Las Vegas, part-time on Maui, she enjoys sitting by the pool with her laptop writing her next spicy romance.

Growing up all she wanted to be was a dancer, actor and author. So far only the latter has come true but M. S. Parker hasn't retired her dancing shoes just yet. She is still waiting for the call to appear on Dancing With The Stars.

When M. S. isn't writing, she can usually be found reading– oops, scratch that! She is always writing.

For more information:
www.msparker.com
msparkerbooks@gmail.com

ACKNOWLEDGMENTS

First, I would like to thank all of my readers. Without you, my books would not exist. I truly appreciate each and every one of you.

A big THANK YOU goes out to all the Facebook fans, street team, beta readers, and advanced reviewers. You are a HUGE part of the success of all my series.

Also thank you to my editor Lynette, my proofreader Nancy, and my wonderful cover designer, Sinisa. You make my ideas and writing look so good.

42184601R00138

Made in the USA
Lexington, KY
13 June 2019